PRESENCE

MERE JOYCE

ORACLE OF SENDERS

FOR THOSE WHO KNOW THE VALUE OF A GOOD GHOST STORY
ON A COLD, DECEMBER NIGHT.

MIM

A little more time. Please just give me a little more time.

My typical prayer, the same one I've made for the past ten years. The same prayer I've uttered since the moment I knew I'd done something blasphemous, despite the lies I told myself to keep the guilt at bay. Once, the lies succeeded in bolstering my self-righteous conviction. But no longer do they placate the nagging pinch of my sins.

Head lowered, I make my prayer and wait for the walls to whisper their comforts, for the reverie of the vaulted ceilings and angelic murals to have its usual effect. Only, it's not usual. Not anymore. Once, this place held miracles for me. But after suffering a dead man's violations, I don't feel the power of this house. I don't feel the power of anything.

I cross myself and rise to my feet, giving up on my worship and accepting the continued thrum of loneliness echoing inside my heart. Making my way back towards the world outside this silent haven, the heels of my flat shoes click over the marbled porcelain floors until they are stayed by the sight of Father Ramírez. His name fills my head and brings the shadow of a smile to my face. Father Ramírez is only ten years my senior. Most of my life, the men I have seen in his uniform are old, withered with age or stern with tradition. But this Father is different.

He almost makes me want to tell him the truth.

"Mim," he says, and I sigh into the slight relief of hearing my name, my *true* name, not the Maria the other Fathers insist on using. "You're here again."

And just like that, the relief is gone. His soft voice cuts like a sharp barb of wire. There is something in his tone that is not quite accusation, but not quite acceptance of my repeat visits, either.

"When you lose a year of your life, you have a lot of prayers to make up for," I say.

Father Ramírez steps closer to me. He has a handsome face, with pronounced angles and wise eyes. Even when he is old, he will not look like the other Fathers I have known. This man will always retain his grace.

"You missed a year of your life," he says. His head tilts to one side, his dark eyes shining. "You should make up for it by living, not by praying for days that have already gone by."

I like the way his voice sounds, even as he is berating me. Quiet, grounded. Like a blanket of moss on the rainforest floor, his words curl and nestle in my ears. But it does not mean his remonstrations strike me as true.

"I have things to atone for," I tell him. My own voice is meek, and I hate how it whimpers from my lips. I used to love listening to myself talk. I used to love a lot of things about myself. What I loathed was so insignificant before. But now that insignificance has enveloped me, taking over everything else.

Father Ramírez steps forward again, though he never allows himself to get too close—never invades the bubble of space I've required since my release from the hospital four months ago. "Mim." My name is a breath from his lungs, worry laced with a passionate hope he can once more make me whole. "You are not to blame for what happened to you. If anything, you survived for a reason. You are strong. And you are proof that miracles do happen—that unyielding faith has its rewards. A community prayed for you while you were in the hospital. Your father prayed for you every single day. And here you are."

He reaches out a hand, and when I don't flinch away his smooth, long fingers brush against my shoulder. "This place is always here, as am I," he says. His fingers tighten just enough so he can shift my body, turning me until I'm facing the back of the altar. "But do not live your life confined within its walls. That is what those doors are for. To let you out into the sun."

He doesn't understand. None of them do. They think what happened to me was an accident, a swimming trip gone wrong when a storm blew in and I hit my head on a stone. They are fools, the lot of them, and I didn't deserve their prayers. The accident was no accident at all. I put myself in that coma because I was stupid. I put my friends in danger because I was so selfish I failed to see the truth.

Just a little more time.

I am still selfish, even now. Even knowing what I do. The Father is good. Handsome, kind, and willing to see past my glaring faults. If he knew what I was, would he still stand at my side? If he knew where I really spent my summers, would he still find me blameless?

I want to warn him against helping me, but the words fail to come. "Okay," is all I manage, before I step away and continue beyond the rows of wooden pews.

"Mim?" Father Ramírez calls after me as I near the door. I look over my shoulder, surprised by how young and jubilant he seems when he smiles. "You should dye your hair again as well," he says. He touches his own lustrous, black locks. "I miss the pink."

I am hollow inside. But even a shell can find herself graced with a blushing smile before she turns into the bright day.

THE SUN IS WARM IN THE PLAZA, DESPITE THE STREET VENDORS I CAN SEE with their piñatas and fireworks reminding me it is December and soon time for La Quema del Diablo. With a final thought to Father Ramírez left behind in the dim candle-glow, I allow the light of the day to sweep against my cheek before I lower my head with a sigh. Telling me to live my life is easy, when the Father doesn't know what I've been responsible for. The lives I've endangered, the souls I've kept hostage. If my neighbors knew the truth, I would become the devil they wanted to burn. I never used to believe my abilities were anything short of divine. But now, the sight of the firecrackers fills me with trepidation. I understand the desire to burn away the unholy. Sometimes, I feel worthy of being burned away too.

"Maria?"

I glance to my left, annoyed by the skulking figure at the side of the road. His secretive stance is like something from a teledrama. I sigh again and pivot on my heel to approach him. He is an older man, his skin dark and his eyes a watery gray. He is not the sort of man I would approach on the street, normally. But the sheen of his blue suit gives away his intentions. This is an Oracle man, and I know exactly why he's here.

"You're ready," I say. It's not a question, and the man offers no other explanation for his sudden appearance. He nods and hands me a slip of folded paper. When I open it, I see an address typed in small, black font.

"We'll meet you there two nights from now. At midnight," he says. His English is worse than mine, but he speaks slow enough I understand. I nod in response, then turn back to the road. A motion behind me, near the church door, hints at the young Father watching the exchange. I don't check to see. I want to pretend he hasn't noticed a thing. The angels only know what he'd think if he has.

Two years ago, teaming up with the Oracle to help release a trapped soul would have been thrilling. Now, it is the only way I can get them off my back. I am done with ghosts. But the Senders won't leave me alone, so I've promised to help them one more time. The smallest sliver of my old pride is flattered by their determination to keep me involved. But their motives can't be so simple as to want me for my talent. They must need to save face by showing whatever power is in charge of the organization that the coma victim is able to bounce back and return to their ranks.

I hope Father Ramírez didn't see the man and his slip of paper. My own father won't let the Oracle near the house, so they're trying to be discreet. But Papa is not home right now, and Mama never minds the company. Not that I could ever let any Senders inside my home. I couldn't attempt anything as risky as that.

A little more time. I just need a little more time.

I clench the paper in my fist, willing the next two days to pass quickly so I can be finished with this task and finished with the Oracle of Senders for good. I believed Anjelo Savou was the last spirit I would ever have a hand in releasing. It annoys me to know that conviction will not hold true. But at least this time I won't wind up stuck alone with the dead. This time, I won't let the dead get inside to eat away at my living spirit.

I leave the plaza and walk through the streets, skirting the vendor stalls and thinking of my last ghostly encounter. I can't remember much from that long ago night in Tonga. The final clear recollection I have is of the wind blowing in the cave, rocks rattling around me, and the wrenching sensation of my chest being peeled open before the spirit of Anjelo Savou squeezed in against my lungs. I wasn't by myself in the cave that night. But in my memory I am the only one there.

Me. And Anjelo.

In what muddled impressions I retain from my time in the hospital, it was just the two of us there as well. Our souls struggled against each other, both of us swallowed by pain, desperation—and eventually, quiet defeat. I sank into an empty place, one as weightless and salty as the sea but far more stagnant and hopeless than the lively waters that rush against the shore. I sank into the abyss of my being, no longer willing to fight and giving in to a fatigued acceptance of my unconscious state.

Until the moment something knocked on my chest

and told me to wake up.

My heart beats faster as I recall how the quiet faded and the desperation returned. How the pain blossomed into something thorny and thick that clogged my throat and tried to keep me from breathing. How the struggle to move sent shivers of aching needles cascading across every inch of my skin. And then there were shadows, noises, and suddenly I wasn't alone anymore because two boys were staring at me in the seconds before they rushed out of my hospital room.

Two boys. One of whom knew more than anyone what needed to be done. If Meander Rhoades, of all people, hadn't spent his time finding a fix… if he hadn't been willing to chance my death in order to save my life…

I smile in spite of myself. To think of all the good people praying for my recovery, when the real answer to their prayers was a boy who was okay with letting me die. Before that coma, I would have hated him for it. But now? Now I understand what true pain is—the kind of pain that runs so deep it's woven into the soul. Now, I agree with his decision. Letting me die was worth the risk. I just can't decide if having me live was the better outcome.

I walk the streets of my city, gripping the paper and wondering if there is any truth to what Father Ramírez said about me surviving for a reason. When I reach the gate to my own house, I stuff the paper into my purse and push away his words as I pull out my keys. Stepping into the house, I hang up my purse, shivering as I retrieve the thick shawl from the hook by the door. The pinprick of pain behind my eyes barely registers as I wrap the soft, pink wool around my shoulders and enter the living room.

"I'm back, Mama," I say, pulling the shawl tight as I slump onto the sofa. I turn on the TV and grab the cream-white yarn, thinking of exorcisms and kind, handsome priests as I loop thread around the hook to resume my crocheting.

THE ADDRESS THE SLEUTH-WANNABE SENDER GAVE ME IS NOT OUR FINAL destination, but it is where we will be departing from. When the allotted day comes, I make the trek to test its length and am appeased to find that the walk from my house is short. My family passes a quiet evening at home, Papa reading the news, me crocheting, and Mama roaming the house before she settles to watch us. At ten, I say goodnight and slink off to my room, hook and yarn still in hand. I work until eleven thirty and pray until eleven forty-five. Then I unlatch my bedroom window and let it swing open so I can shimmy over the tiled ledge and drop onto the earth below.

The motion of falling, landing, and breathing in the fresh evening air flushes me with the heat of memory. Once, I did this by myself in order to explore a nearby haunting. At that time, I had been proud of my cunning and thrilled by the prospect of lurking through the dark streets in the danger of the blackened night. Now, a hint of that same excitement tickles my skin like a feather-stroke. But when I swallow, the sensation vanishes and is replaced by the stolid certainty of what I am about to do.

And the ache of knowing it will be my last time doing so.

I head through my neighbors' properties, avoiding the road until I'm forced to cross it. The streets are quiet, and I wander them in silence, my soft-soled shoes padding like the paws of a cat. When I see the light shining in the doorway of a yellow house, I know it is meant for me. I brace myself, lingering with the temptation to turn back before pushing forward into the light's glow.

A woman is waiting for me. Her familiar face shines under the pale light as I step into the yard.

"Mim. It's so good to see you," Mrs. Buxley says.

I hadn't expected to recognize anyone on this outing, but my old camp instructor stands before me with steady eyes and shimmering lips, her high heels out of place on the home's rickety porch.

"I—" I fumble, unsure how to respond.

Mrs. Buxley nods as if the single word was an entire greeting in and of itself. "We should get going," she says before I have time to stammer out a proper, half-hearted 'hello'.

Swooping forward, she takes my arm, cutting off my chance to backpedal on my intentions. I let her hand grasp my skin, her warm presence a rock I didn't realize I needed. A strange sensation—a tumultuous tumble of unease, relief, and peculiar interest—roil together in my belly. Mrs. Buxley makes this endeavor feel less like a publicity stunt. Having her here makes me uncomfortably aware of how well-suited I am to late night excursions such as this.

Was suited. I am not fit for this work anymore. That's not the girl I am now.

I allow Mrs. Buxley to lead me to the black car parked across the street. We both slide into the backseat, and I see there are two others waiting up front. The driver is a younger woman with a long curtain of sleek brown hair. From the back, she reminds me of Kornelía, though when she turns around her face is pocked and creased, hints of a sarcastic personality shining through in place of Kornelía's serene one.

I sigh, wishing my friend was here. Although I suppose if she was, she wouldn't be in the driver's seat. Kornelía used to send me emails every week, but now that she requires her brother to dictate the messages because her eyesight is too poor to read the screen, the letters are less frequent and infinitely less transparent and real. I guess I'm not the only one who has churned through hellish waters in their quest to become a Sender. I'd wager my experience is worse than hers, but it will probably prove to be shorter. One year is nothing, if I go on living. But Korni isn't likely to get her full eyesight back anytime soon.

The other person in the car is the man who gave me the slip of paper two days ago. He offers me a solitary nod before facing forward as not-Kornelía starts the engine.

"Is there anything you'd like to know, regarding the case?" Mrs. Buxley asks.

I stare out the window, pretending I can see every building we pass. "A fifteen-year-old girl," I recite, the case details memorized as soon as I agreed to this last Sender-driven venture into the spirit world. "She was promised a dream by a boy who only wanted her family's money. She stole it so they could run away. He took it, used her, abused her, and then left her to die. She did."

For a long moment the car is silent. Then Mrs. Buxley speaks again. "Do you have anything you'd like to ask?"

I turn away from the window and meet my former instructor's gaze. "Why do you need me?"

The hint of a smile graces Mrs. Buxley's lips. It's the question she was hoping to hear and, despite my best intentions to expend no emotions during this trial, I am glad I've passed her private test.

"She is broken," Mrs. Buxley says. "She still feels the pain of her loss. She will not communicate with a man, nor a grown woman. Someone closer to her own age is needed to gain her trust. Someone who understands her pain is needed to help her move on."

"I've never been..." The words hang unfinished as I realize what Mrs. Buxley means. I've never been broken by a living boy. But I've been violated by a dead one.

It hadn't occurred to me that this task would be picked to coincide with my trauma. If I can see the spirit, it means that the girl is broken-hearted. But there are many different ways for a heart to break, and this girl's story—as wholly different from my experience as it may be—bears an unsettling resemblance to my own suffering. Mrs. Buxley would have known that when she chose this as my final ghost. But did she really believe dragging me back into the world of Senders with such a tragic tale would pull at my heartstrings and make me long for Camp Wanagi once more?

No. If my old instructor were not involved in this mission, I would assume that was exactly the intent of tonight. But Mrs. Buxley is not stupid. If she allowed this choice, there is a more logical reason for it.

We drive down the empty streets that tomorrow evening will be full of bonfires as children delight in the snaps of the firecrackers, and the most superstitious of the adults cling to the idea that they are truly burning away the evil of the past year. Perhaps *that* is the point of this mission—to burn away the evil of my past. If only that was how it worked. If only this one good deed could erase all of my foolish mistakes. But life is not so simple. I suppose death isn't, either.

My fingers shake, and I curse myself for not bringing along my yarn. I clench my hands into fists and press them against my thighs, turning away from the window and the black world outside.

THE HOUSE, WITH ITS SHORT, STONE WALLS COVERED BY A PARTIALLY
collapsed tin roof, is more hut than home. What once
constituted a yard is now a mass of dead grass and
thin, reedy weeds. The girl—I'm told her name is
Beatriz—died twenty-two years ago. A dozen families
have lived in the house since then, some dying off,
some moving to better places, some simply shuffling
along to try their fortune elsewhere. The Oracle was
not contacted by the house's owners, tenants desperate
to rid their happy abode of the restless dead. No one
would care about a spirit residing here. Ghosts are
expected in places like this.

I envisioned a high-profile case, a persistent landlord
or someone with rich ties willing to pay whatever was
necessary to rid their home of a peculiar pest. But this
release will not be attempted for the sake of some
well-paying or well-tortured client. Releases made in
hollow, rotted places like these are done solely for the

sake of the suffering soul caged inside.

The sight of the house pulls at *something* in me, something less brittle than my heart. Maybe the Oracle does need my help. Maybe Mrs. Buxley is telling the truth, and there's no way the other three Senders here could do this job without my assistance.

My chest constricts as strained eagerness swells under my lungs. I used to ache to be necessary, used to pine for each chance to prove myself a leader. But that's not me anymore. And yet—that doesn't mean I can't help. This one last time. The brash girl I used to be is gone. But maybe the wisdom her folly brought can help another girl who is already dead and not yet gone at all.

"Mrs. Buxley," I start.

"Eniola," Mrs. Buxley corrects.

The name stops my tongue, the act of informality so strange it almost makes me laugh. Almost. I haven't laughed in over a year, not since I was in Tonga. If I even laughed then. I can't really remember.

"Eniola," I say after a careful pause. The pretty name brings a soft smile to my lips. "Do you really think I will be able to help?"

"Why would I ask you to come, if I didn't?" she replies before opening the door and stepping out into the night.

I stay in the car for several long seconds, waiting for the panic to set in. It seems inevitable, a mandatory element for this final task. But it doesn't come. My anxieties have never been related to the ghosts themselves. The only fears I have held within my breast are fears of failure. But I have nothing to prove tonight, and that simple fact keeps me calm. I am not afraid of the dead. I am only afraid of confirming the worst suspicions I have about myself. That I am weak. That I am ineffective. That I am wholly, incomprehensibly selfish. I don't want to be at this broken house tonight. But if I help the girl inside, perhaps it will shave a little of the fear off my bones.

I cast a long look at the glassless windows of the hut before I exit the car. Mrs. Buxley—Eniola—leads the way towards the house. I trail behind her, while the others bring up the rear. They don't carry any equipment, aside from a single battery-powered lantern that the wannabe-sleuth holds in one, outstretched hand. It feels as though we are unprepared, except that I suspect these people have everything under total control. No researching is needed tonight, no extra precautions to try and ward off the possibility of irreparable damage. These are professionals, not a bunch of teenagers pretending they know what they're doing.

I remember the first spirit I helped to release. I forget her name, as I've forgotten a lot since I woke from my coma. But I remember her floating in a hotel room in France. I remember her pain. I remember her pleas. And I remember the five clueless Shades scrambling to figure out what they were supposed to do to make her go away.

My lips twitch and my heart patters.

I cross the threshold into the hut.

5

THE MAN HOLDING THE LANTERN WAITS FOR ME TO ENTER THE HOUSE FIRST. With the light to my back, the first few steps into the hut are black. I rake in a breath, trying not to recall the last time darkness engulfed me—the first time I recognized blackness as a tangible thing. Waves crash in my ears, and the skin on my arms turns to gooseflesh. I bite down against a whimper, but I cannot keep my foot from backing away from the lack of light. I retreat until my shoulder hits the man, and he holds the lantern higher to illuminate the space.

The halo of artificial light pushes the darkness back, and the solid reminder of my living company helps to quiet the noise in my ears. I take a deeper breath and continue into the hut, glancing around at the rubble left within. There are scraps of old clothes, plastic bottles, and a few bits of sheet metal from whoever was here last. Dust and pebbles are scattered throughout, and at the light's presence bugs swarm into the recesses of the chipped stone walls.

"She's back here," Eniola says. The older woman steps gracefully, her heels never stumbling on the pebbles, her balance never put off by the dimness of the house. We pass through the main room, as well as a small space I imagine was once a bedroom, although now there is no roof to protect it from rain. I'm determined to stay uninvested in this case, but I can't help yearning for facts about the house, like knowing how the roof caved in. During a storm? In the cold? With a family sleeping beneath its failing cover? Beatriz appears to be the only ghost in residence. But that doesn't mean hers is the only tragedy to occur within these crumbling walls.

I don't want to care about the people who once called this their home. I don't have time to care, even if I did. I'm here for one reason, and that reason is beckoning me closer. My skin is still raised rough and bumpy, and the air is growing steadily cooler as we walk farther into the house. The sensation of getting colder doesn't bother me. But the gentle pain, along with the rhythmic thudding in my head that amplifies with each step, makes it harder to keep up the façade of disinterest.

The man with the lantern and the woman who drove us here linger behind as we pick through the house. My eyes sweep over each room before they settle on the familiar sight of my old instructor as she leads me on. When the air is thoroughly chilled and the thudding is louder than my own thoughts, we approach an open doorway. I expect Eniola to pause on the threshold of the final room in the hut's back corner. I expect her to turn around and face me, to ask me one last time if I am ready for what we are about to see. But she steps into the room as if there's no ghost within it—as if there is nothing unusual about this hut at all.

She doesn't stop. So neither do I.

WHEN I WALK INTO THE CRAMPED, LOW-CEILINGED ROOM, THE COLD swoops down from above. It's like standing in the street and being assaulted by the ravages of a sudden downpour. A chill cascades from my hairline to my toes, and I shiver, clutching my arms to my chest and shutting my eyes against the noise in my head.

Thud. Thud. Thud. Thud. Thud.

A heartbeat that doesn't belong to me hammers in my brain, and I squint against its pressure as I shuffle into the center of the space. I don't dare move my head to survey my surroundings, lest I be lashed with a sharp jolt of pain. But the hut is small enough I don't need to swivel about to know the ghost is not yet visible. The room is cold but empty. My head, on the other hand, is full of her dead heart and—soon enough—her dead words as well.

"Go away," she whispers, the sound tinny and scared. *"Please, go away."*

With a hard swallow, I slide my eyes to Eniola, looking for guidance I do not receive. My former instructor stares at me, waiting for my reaction. She's too used to the old Mim, the girl I was before Anjelo dug his nails into my soul. Now, I don't want to react. I don't want to be here at all.

Eniola does not take her eyes off of me, but while her expression remains neutral, I detect a hint of expectation in the gentle slope of her shimmering mouth. Annoyance strikes against the thudding in my head, and for a flashing second I long to meet her challenge and take everyone by surprise with my superior ability. But flashes are short, and the desire is snuffed out faster than a candle's flame. What I would like most of all right now is to hide in my home or—given the pain already in my head—in the silent warmth of the church. But I cannot flee to the quiet safety of my passionless faith until this ghost is released. I must help her, or I must prove to everyone here that I can't.

"We come with peaceful intentions," I say as I blink away from Eniola to gaze around the rest of the room. The ghost does not materialize, but the pounding in my head grows louder. "We're not going to hurt you." The words sound insincere as they dissipate into the darkness of the shadowed room, my voice as hollow as the rest of me. I draw in an icy breath and try to make the emotion more genuine. "Please, Beatriz. Tell me what I can do to help you. You don't need to be afraid. I'm going to make everything all right."

I wait for a response that doesn't come, and then I offer Eniola a shrug. The statuesque lady does not even blink. She watches me, waiting for me to attempt another angle. The annoyance strikes again, but I push it away in favor of looking at the space around me. Turning on my heel, I spin in a slow circle, studying the small square illuminated by the lantern shining outside of the room. All I see are dirt floors, stone walls, and the edges where the roof has been destroyed.

The place is a slum that can barely even be called a shelter. I don't know what the exact state of this house was when Beatriz died here. But it wasn't nice. I'm certain of that much. It was a slum back then, and Beatriz was not treated well while within its dubious hold.

I don't want to imagine her curled on the floor of this room, waiting for a lover that eventually came with greedy plans in his heart. But I do. I've seen a photo of the girl, and I know she was younger than I am now when her life was taken from her. She was as young as I was the last time I attended camp, when I, too, had a boy who didn't treat me well.

My smile comes unexpectedly, amused as I am by the solemn realization that before the summer in Tonga, I never actually knew what it was to be heartbroken. Not in that way. Not because of a cute boy with wild eyes and a carefree mind. When I first met Dylan Benowitz in France, I thought he was a fun plaything, something to keep close for whenever I was bored and in need of entertainment. I was bad to him, and a year later, he was bad to me. Yet Dylan's betrayal was nothing compared to what Beatriz faced. My heart took a beating from that boy, but he would never have stolen my money, my body—my life.

Beatriz didn't deserve what happened to her. And the boy that took her life didn't deserve to get away. I never used to think anyone's actions truly warranted pain. But now I know better. My naivety is gone. Some of my purity has vanished too.

I crouch down low and drag my fingers through the dust on the floor, wondering if this was where Beatriz lay, screaming and begging for her lover to spare her the agony of death. I close my eyes, holding back a sob of pity for a girl I never knew. My hand scrapes into a fist, and dust rains between my fingers as a scowl crosses my lips. I listen to the pounding in my head, and slowly, I open my eyes.

To see Beatriz staring at me.

I fall back, startled by her sudden appearance. The pounding continues, and a smell—of blood and dirt co-mingled—makes me gag. I cover my mouth with the back of my hand, staring at the vaporous ghost before me. Her hair is a straggled mass, and there are foggy patches of emptiness against her head that I suspect is where hair was ripped from her scalp. Her eyes are wide, indented formations so vivid I can almost see the eyelashes. Her mouth is small, her nose flat, her neck long. She is skinny and short, as short as I am. She is sad and desperate. She is scared.

And so am I.

"*Let me go*," the ghost says. I don't know if she's talking to me or to the boy who left her in this unholy place, but when she reaches a hand out towards me, I scramble back, fearful of her touch. Talking to ghosts is one thing. But I never want to touch the dead again.

I gain my footing and stand, my steps retreating until I hit the stone wall.

"*Let me go*," the girl pleads. Her hands grab for me, and I gasp-sob, unable to keep the bloom of panic at bay.

"I can't do this," I say to her. To everyone.

I rush out of the room, crashing into the Sender holding the lantern on the far side of the door. With another sob, I push past him and run through the rest of the house.

7

side. I'm wracked with sensations I didn't think I knew how to feel anymore, and my body retaliates in shocked surprise with dry, painful heaves. I will be sore tomorrow from the muscle spasms. Between the shivering and retching, I have to work hard to remember to breathe.

Once, I longed for these moments. Connecting with spirits used to provide me with unparalleled joy. The first time I released a ghost on my own, the bleary waking moments post-release were like waking up on a heavenly cloud. I felt invincible and utterly confirmed in my belief that my gifts were divinely bestowed. My physical self was tired, but my soul thrived with the happy conviction of what I could do.

I don't feel that way any longer. Or at least, I don't feel it to the same extent. Crouching next to the car, I pull my rosary from under my shirt and grip the cross tight. It would be foolish of me to deny the gift I've been given. Because I am still sure that it is, in fact, a gift. There are those who would disagree, who have always disagreed with the peculiar way I behaved as a child when I insisted I could speak with the dead. Some of the people in my neighborhood believed I was possessed by a demon. When I was eight, one old crow even suggested I get exorcised.

The memory brings a rueful smile to my lips, even while tears fill my eyes and drip down my cheeks. If only she knew. If only anyone really knew. I have been pried apart. But it did not expose some hidden demonic force. There were four souls involved in the exorcism that brought me back. One dead. Two living. And me stuck somewhere in between. Not a demon among us.

I have never been hounded by something demonic. Even Anjelo, furious as he was, could not be called such a vile thing. And he was only inside because of my own mistakes, not because of something thrust on me by powers beyond my control. My gift *is* a gift, and no one will ever make me think otherwise. But as much as I believe the gift was bestowed for a purpose greater than my simple, mortal being could possibly comprehend, it doesn't change the fact that I'm not sure if I can still go on using it.

Tonight is a test. I know the truth of that, but it doesn't make things easier. I don't feel the presence of the angels anymore. I am alone. And I'm not sure how to handle that.

I close my eyes and think of Beatriz. I do not picture her as the ghost I just encountered but rather as the girl from the photo I was shown when the Oracle slipped me her file. I imagine her huddled in the house, barely clinging to life and all alone through the last moments before her death. I am alone in how I feel tonight. But the girl was alone at the end of her life, and now she will continue to be alone forever—until someone gets her out of this horrible place.

"Mim?"

I open my eyes to see Eniola standing before me. She does not look disappointed to find me squatting next to the car. She does not look surprised, either. She only looks like Mrs. Buxley, the ever-steady instructor from camp who always knows more than I do.

Kornelía does not email me much these days. But she writes me often enough that I know what has happened since I left Tonga in a comatose state. I know what occurred last summer before I came to—and after. I know Shade is smaller now by two members. One who left the Oracle by her parents' will, and one who left by the ending of his own life.

Mrs. Buxley was there the evening Reed Vodden died. And she was the one to help him after he became a ghost.

"Do you ever wonder if you can keep doing what you do?" I ask. A tear rolls onto my lips as I talk, its salt stinging my tongue as I lick it away.

"I don't," Eniola Buxley says. She considers me for a long moment. Then she nods. "I don't allow myself to wonder. Because I don't have a choice. This talent was given to me. I suspect I will never fully understand why. But I do know that I have a responsibility to help this world in whatever way I can. This is the way I can help the most." She pauses, then adds, "when it comes to how *you* can help... that is a decision you must make for yourself."

I think about the months I spent in a coma, loose fragments of remembered time that felt like lying at the edge of existence, teetering in a murky abyss of confusion and suffocating dullness. I always wanted to be special. And because of my own failings, I have gained what I desired most. I am unlike any of the other Senders-in-training that I have met. Because I know what it is like to be a ghost. I understand just how agonizing this world is when you're not equipped to live in it.

"No," I say with a quiet breath. "It's not. I don't have a choice any more than you do." I grip my cross so tight it threatens to cut into my skin. The tears stay on my cheeks as I stand. "Leave me alone with Beatriz," I say. "I will help her move on."

THE MAN TRIES TO LEAVE THE LANTERN, BUT I REFUSE THE OFFER OF LIGHT.
The darkness terrifies me. But terrified is how I need
to be just now. After making my intentions clear, the
adults nod their heads and bid me good luck. I wait
for Eniola and the other two Senders to leave the hut,
watching as the light fades until only the vaguest
impressions of the moon's cold glow filter in from the
open windows. Trembling, I force myself to breathe
deep—not to stop the shaking but to make it bearable.
When I'm somewhat under control, I go back to
Beatriz's room.

"I'm here," I say as soon as the noise of her heartbeat
starts in my head.

Thud. Thud. Thud.

The shiver falls over me again as Beatriz materializes
before my face. I can read her emotions easily, even
through the foggy filter of death. She is broken, scared,
and still in disbelief about what happened all those

years ago. I allow her worries to press into me, allow myself to feel the whole of her fractured half-existence. Every second of her companionship is painful. But I don't flinch away from what she brings.

I clutch at the threads of betrayal streaming from her mass. But much thicker are the strands of desperation that wrap her body like a smoky shroud. My sticky eyes widen with surprise, and I, too, become cloaked as its cold truth settles over me. She is desperate, but not because she longs for release. If that were the case, she would have already left. The first ghost I helped release, that woman floating in the hotel room in France, wanted people to know the truth about her betrayal. But I soon understand that is not what Beatriz is hoping for, either.

"You want him back," I say after a moment.

The ghost nods, and the thudding in my heart grows louder as the cold seeps deeper beneath my skin.

She wants to be back with the boy who betrayed her.

I'm shocked into silence until the mist in my head shifts and I'm able to stretch out the denial coiled beneath the longing. She wants the boy back not because she loves him in spite of what he did. She wants him back because she is trying, even now, to pretend he never did it.

"You've convinced yourself he was someone he wasn't," I say. I crouch down, then give up and sit flat on the ugly, dirty floor. "Because the truth is too hard for you to accept."

I understand her plight, perhaps a little too well. And that makes me angry. Because suddenly I know why it is the Senders truly sent me here, a motive that has nothing to do with what happened in Tonga.

I am not talking to Beatriz because we share similar situations. We are together now because of our similar delusions. Beatriz can't face the truth. I always have. But I've long denied the inevitable *resolution* of my truth. Of my secret.

Just a little more time.

The annoyance comes, and this time I let it linger. The heated anger settles over me like a flame, hot but comforting as it lights my way. I have pity for this girl and the horrible past she endured. But I do not pity her denial of what she experienced. I've never denied what happened to me. *None* of the things that have happened to me. If I could, maybe I would pretend I was never possessed by a spirit who burrowed into my body and nearly took my life. But I can't pretend that. Anjelo was with me in the most intimate sense possible, completely without my consent. I gave him permission to come into me. I never gave him permission to stay.

Perhaps I would pretend nothing happened, if I could. Perhaps I would also pretend the other tragedies of my life never occurred. But that was not the fate given to me. And I will not let it be Beatriz's fate, either.

I look up at the ghost who is hovering over my head, distant but curious at my presence in her house.

"He doesn't love you," I say with as much flat certainty as I can muster.

The ghost's eyes brighten, the mass filling in with a whipping crackle of fury at what I've said. Her stubborn anger is like an echo of my own former temperament, and the familiarity of its snapping arrival motivates me to keep going. Never before have

I been rude to a spirit. I revere the dead. Or I did, until Anjelo. I am less awed by their existence now. Yet, that doesn't mean I am happy to say such nasty things to a girl I never knew. Heartbreak is horrible, in whatever form it takes. She didn't deserve it. I used to believe no one did.

I climb to my knees as the girl's anger grows and the first pinches of discomfort ripple through my stomach. I'm good at handling the sickening swell of being near the dead. Since my coma, I've become an absolute professional at it. If my fellow Shades were here, some of them would be doubled over, moaning in pain and clutching their mouths to keep the bile at bay. I don't feel any of that now. A little pain in the head. A little turmoil in my gut. That's all.

But that's enough. I don't want to be here. And neither does Beatriz. I cannot give her the happy ending she desires. But I can provide one that's better than the fantasy she's clung to even after death.

"He doesn't love you," I say again. But although my words are sour, I hold my arms out in welcome, as if I'm willing to embrace her despite how much I fear her possible touch. "But I can grant you love. He used you. He took everything you had. Everything except for one last choice. You can stay here and mourn the boy who does not mourn you. Or you can listen to what I say and go to the lightness that is full of love."

The ghost's crackling anger curbs as the bitterness of my words dissolve into the sweetness of my offer. She hovers a little closer to me, waiting to hear more of what I have to say.

"There is goodness away from this place. Away from this pain. You were taken from your life so that you could escape the horror of it. You struggled and stayed, and that was wrong. But you can make it right. Go to the light, Beatriz. Go away from here. And let him go too."

The spirit's heart is hammering in my head, scared but also full of a hope she hasn't felt in a long time. The words I've offered her are nothing extraordinary. But perhaps no one has said them before. Or perhaps she's only listening now because she can sense how well I understand the agony her denial brings. "Go, Beatriz. I will stay with you until you are gone. I promise you will suffer no more pain. He will never come back for you. But you can save yourself and leave it all behind."

The ghost studies me in a way no spirit ever has, scrutinizing as she considers what choice she should make. Her body could not withstand what that boy did to her. But her mind is surprisingly fierce, even in death. I appreciate the clarity of her thoughts as she hovers closer still to my body. She stares so intently into my eyes I'm almost fooled into believing she's alive.

"*No pain?*" she asks in a small, bewildered voice.

I close my eyes, lifting my chin towards her as I smile. "No pain," I promise with the whole of my damaged soul.

Even with my eyes closed, I know when her arms reach out. For the slightest second there is a frozen stab of pain as she touches me. I withstand her touch, holding myself still and keeping my heart open until the pain softens and morphs until it is no more than the happy ache of a bright, glowing light. The thudding in my head steadies, and when it begins to sync with my own pulse, I know she is ready to leave. She takes my energy in waves, and I crumple slowly, careful not to hit my head on the hard ground. My eyes stay closed through it all, and I keep smiling as the peace of the release washes over me—a peace I have not felt in nearly two years.

I WAKE IN THE BACKSEAT OF THE BLACK CAR. I DON'T KNOW HOW MUCH TIME has passed, but it can't have been long. The sky is still dark as the car drives through streets I suspect are close to my home.

"She's gone," I mumble, still half-asleep and not entirely certain if any of this is more than a dream. I'm used to that feeling. During my time with Anjelo, I lived permanently in such a state, forever wondering if anything in my life had been real or if the hazy nothing was my only true reality.

But when Eniola speaks, her voice—as solid as the car's interior—brings me back to the living world.

"Yes, she is," my instructor says. "Thank you for your assistance."

She does not praise the swiftness of the release, which I am grateful for. Once, I wanted always to be praised. Now, I understand that I am not worthy of it. The job I completed was the one I was meant to do. It is not something I need to be fawned over for.

I try not to change the tense in my head, but I can't help the shift from 'was' to 'am'. It is a job I *am* meant to do. I wanted to give it up. But that's not possible. If I was supposed to give it up, my talent would not have simply stagnated while I was in a coma. It would have disappeared altogether. *I* would have disappeared altogether.

I fought against the truth because I wanted to forget the pain of my past. But the past can be far more haunting than an actual ghost, and Beatriz reminded me of what's truly missing in the life I've created for myself.

Peace. And purpose.

I sit up and look at Eniola.

"My ability," I say, the thoughts working their way slowly from my mind to my mouth as I translate them into the English we use to communicate. "It is no different now than it was before."

I don't mean before the coma. I mean before my birthday, the one I passed in a hospital room with flowers on my bedside that I could not see or smell.

Eniola understands. "I cannot say anything with certainty," she tells me. "But I suspect the struggle you underwent while in that coma put your abilities in stasis. Your body expended all of its energy trying to keep you intact." I like that she doesn't say *alive*. It wasn't only life I was fighting for when Anjelo and I shared a vessel. "Whatever development you would likely have undergone as you matured has been dampened."

It's punishment. I don't say so aloud, but I know it's true. If I hadn't been so self-centered, so convinced of my own immense strength and capability, I would not have endured the fate I did. I was graced with continued life. And continued use of my talent. But my ability will never gain any new depths. I will never mature into a fully-developed Sender.

I am not bitter about the turn my life has taken. In this moment, I am only grateful for the realization that it is not as faded as I've lately believed. Thus far, my awakening has been hollow. But after tonight I know it will not be hollow anymore. I suspect it will never be as fiercely passionate as it once was. But I have no desire to rebel against the punishment I have been given. Meekness suits me better than I expected. I will revere and respect the ability I have. But no longer will I seek attention and fame for the talents bestowed upon me.

"We're at your home," Eniola says a few minutes later. She touches my hair and stirs me from my thoughts. "Would you like help to get back inside?"

My legs are heavy and prickling with sleep. But I shake my head.

"I am fine. Thank you." I look at my instructor and nod. "Thank you."

Eniola nods as well, and I open the door to climb out into the night. Before I shut it behind me, she calls my name.

"Mim." The warmth of the word catches my ear, and I spin to face her. Eniola smiles, the curve of her lips slight but meaningful. "I'll see you in the summer."

She does not ask if I intend to return to Camp Wanagi. She doesn't have to. I give her another nod. Then I shut the door and walk carefully back to my window.

I CLIMB THROUGH THE WINDOW AND SLIP INTO MY ROOM UNNOTICED. Almost unnoticed. The room is cold when I pad across the floor and crawl under the heavy blankets of my bed. I close my eyes against the dull, pricking hammer as Mama enters the room. Grasping the blankets tight, I shiver and burrow more deeply into the vague promise of warmth, keeping my back to the door where she stands. For a long time, we are both silent, and I almost drift back into the wave of weariness brought on by Beatriz's release. Almost drift. I can't quite let myself go while I know she is watching me. Once, her presence was a comfort I believed I could never be without. Now, she is a constant reminder of everything I've done wrong.

"*Mim?*"

I do not answer her, at first. I stare at the wall and will her to leave my room, but she doesn't budge. She never does. So eventually, I roll onto my back with a sigh that ripples through every crease in my mind and soul.

"I love you, Mama," I say into the night. My head is tight with the sound of thudding. I ignore it the way I always ignore the constant nag of pain. "I'm almost ready to do what I need to." Almost unnoticed. Almost drifting. Almost ready. "A few more months. One more summer. Then I will do it. I promise, Mama. I do."

Mama says nothing. She never says much more than my name anymore. I didn't like the things she used to tell me. So, somewhere along the way, she stopped telling them.

A tear leaks from the corner of my eye, and I let it roll along the curve of my cheek as I turn my head.

"I just need a little more time," I whisper.

The blue-white smoke of the mother who died ten years ago stares back at me, silent and waiting for the day my promises will finally come true.

DYLAN

Dennis laughs, the stupid laugh he does that sounds more like someone suffering an onslaught of asthma. I give him the finger and keep up my current pace.

Of all the cousins I had to spend my holiday with, why these two? Dennis, the only one of the Benowitz clan who goes to the same school as I do. And Roddy, the only one idiotic enough to think visiting an abandoned amusement park in the middle of the night is a good way to spend Hanukkah.

"Roddy, it's freezing," Chastity, the single highlight to this crappy evening, says. Well, she would be a highlight, if she wasn't dating Roddy and if I hadn't been introduced as Sludge. She's gorgeous, all curves with long black hair and warm brown skin that makes my reflection look like I've just stepped out of a newspaper comic.

"We'll be there soon, babe," Roddy says in his typical

asshole fashion. "It's right up that ridge."

Up that ridge. As if we haven't been walking up the side of this stupid hill for half an hour already. If the night were nice, maybe it wouldn't be so bad. But it started raining before we even got out of the car, and the damn air is so cold the wet's just a couple of degrees off from turning to snow.

I stomp forward, overzealous in my irritation. My foot slides down the grass, and I nearly fall flat on my face. Would, if Chastity didn't step back and grab my arm to steady me while my cousins snicker.

"You okay?" she asks.

I'd make some kind of comment that could double as a come on, if I didn't suspect she was only helping me because she thinks I'm dying. Most people do when they first meet me. My mother's still half-convinced, and I've looked this way for nearly a year.

"I'm fine," I grumble instead. I'm not in the mood for flirting, even if I did think it might get me somewhere. It's one in the morning, and I'm supposed to be fast asleep, stuffed full of loukoumades with Roddy's golden retriever curled up at the end of my bed. I should be warm and content, not cold and pissed off. This is supposed to be a vacation. Not some lousy expedition with my idiot cousins who actually think this is cool.

"We're here," Roddy says a few minutes later. He crosses his arms over his chest and surveys the area with a smug grin. "Look. Ain't she a beauty?"

"This is so awesome," Dennis pipes in. Dennis sucks up, more like. He's fourteen and thinks Roddy's some big action hero because he's seventeen and knows how to drive—barely. I'm only a year younger, but

Dennis has never looked at me like that. I guess the gray kid who's always hanging around dogs doesn't earn the same kind of respect.

"I don't know, Roddy," Chastity says when we crest the hill and look at the dump of old metalwork swirling into the night. "This seems dangerous."

"Don't worry, babe," Roddy says. He puts his arm around her shoulder, and she hugs into his side like he's a teddy bear she can cuddle. It makes me sick. But it'd be shitty of me not to admit that's only because I wish *I* was the teddy bear. I'm better equipped for the task. Small guys are way easier to cuddle than tall, broad-shouldered hulks like Roddy.

My cousins and Chastity head into the park, while I linger at the top of the hill. When he realizes I'm not following, Roddy throws a glance over his shoulder and scoffs—as if the very sight of me has personally offended him.

"You coming Dylan?" he asks. "Or are you too afraid?"

I don't want to come. But hell if I'm going to let him think me a coward. Roddy knows nothing about fear. He's never seen his girlfriend in a coma. He's never watched a friend die.

He's never spent whole nights communicating with ghosts.

"What would I be afraid of?" I say, and I'm pleased to hear that my voice is successfully dismissive. "This place is a junk yard. There's nothing here but a couple of idiots who think they're explorers."

I force my legs to take longer strides so I can catch up with everyone else. I'm not going back down that hill in this weather. So, I might as well save what little face I can and keep pace with the others. Chastity, at least, looks impressed by my moxie. Good. Maybe she'll realize there are better guys than Roddy around.

My stomach squirms with the thought, loukoumades and the pretzels I've been shoving in my face all day sloshing around in a subtle reminder that I'm not exactly one of the "better" guys. I'm pining after this stranger when I've already got a girl of my own. Two girls, actually. Which just makes my stomach hurt worse. Two girls, but neither of them people I've talked to in a while. Korni didn't even answer my last email back in October. And Mim—I haven't spoken to Mim in about a year and a half.

What a mess my life has become. Two girlfriends who don't actually want anything to do with me. A complexion so horrendous my parents think I've got one foot permanently in the grave. And two stupid cousins who know nothing, but somehow think I'm the clueless loser of the group.

Sometimes, being a Sender sucks.

"Man, I'm starting to understand why people call you Sludge," Roddy says from way up in front. "Get a move on. We don't have all night!"

I lift my middle finger for the second time in the past fifteen minutes. Then I zip my pylon orange windbreaker and hurry my ass so they'll stop badgering me.

Despite his boasting, Roddy's terrified of getting caught. So instead of walking through the main gates, we enter the park from the side by shimmying under a broken fence. So much for keeping my new coat clean. I swear at my cousins while I wiggle forward under the poking twists of metal. I don't shut my mouth until I'm back on my feet and staring at the shadowed park in front of us.

Our entry point is right next to the park's main attraction, a yellow-tracked coaster that loops over the side of the ridge and at one point offered impressive views of the hillside below. It's a shame the park went under. The coaster would have been an awesome ride on a warm, sunny day. Or even on a dark night if the rain were gone and I was here with my friends.

Friends. I'm not even sure that's the right word for the companions I wish were here. My fellow Shades are much different from me. If I met them at a party, most of us probably wouldn't even make eye contact.

But they're more than camp mates. They're my people. They get what no one else does. Even among them, I'm different. I don't see their ghosts, and they don't see mine. But *everyone* in the Oracle is different. And when I'm at Camp Wanagi, I don't feel like the one who's drawn the short straw in more ways than my height. At least I'm conscious. I can see fine. And I'm not always getting the shit kicked out of me by the dead.

I climb over a second fence next to the coaster, misjudging my step again and landing hard on my knees. Perhaps I'm not *always* getting hurt. But I've got to be more careful if I don't want to end up in a full body cast by the time this stupid excursion is done with.

"Woah, this place is sick," Dennis says. He stares into the night like he's some kind of poet looking for inspiration. A little ways to my left, he leans over the safety railing, lifting onto his toes so he can see way down the slope. "Think anyone's ever died here?"

Roddy punches his side. "No, you loser," he says.

"What?" Dennis asks. "It's a legitimate question. That drop is wicked."

"If someone had died here, I'd know about it," Roddy replies.

"Right, cause you're the keeper of the theme park crypt," I mutter.

"Shut it, Dylan," Roddy says. He scowls and then looks at the park behind me. "Come on. Let's check it out."

He shoves me on his way by, and even though I'm expecting it, I'm still unable to hold my ground against his bulk. Damn muscle mass. I could run circles around Roddy. But he's still the strong one among us. I'm not so pathetic I want my own bodyguard. But if

Sefa were here, Roddy might shut his mouth and stop being such an ass.

Chastity walks behind Roddy and glances at me as she passes. Her smooth face is full of concern, but her pity is almost palpable, and it makes me even more disgruntled. She probably thinks Roddy was forced to bring the dying relative along for one last night of *living*.

"How come the park closed?" Dennis asks as we walk through the zigzagging path that once marked out the line-up for the coaster. "This place is awesome."

Roddy shrugs. "Too far off the road, I guess," he says. "Too much upkeep for the rides."

"I heard this coaster broke a couple of times," Chastity adds. She shakes her head at Dennis's hopeful expression. "I don't think anyone was hurt, though."

Dennis's face falls. As if he's really hoping to uncover a grisly secret about this place. People love ghastly tales. I don't get it. I've never once gone to an abandoned kennel in hopes of discovering horrific crimes committed against innocent dogs.

Not that I've ever been to an abandoned kennel. I wonder if there is such a thing. Might be a good place for communication. I should check it out once I'm home. I've gotten pretty good at scouting potential haunting grounds now. Being able to actually communicate with my dead has helped a lot. I remember thinking Mim was crazy when she confessed to releasing ghosts on her own. But I understand now. Being a ghost has got to suck. And it's not like my social calendar is brimming. My mother won't even let me get an after-school job for fear it'll "worsen my condition". I've got a lot of spare time on my hands. Helping dogs is a good way to fill the hours.

"Yo!" I walk into something solid and blink away from my thoughts to see that the something is Roddy. "What the hell is your problem? You're not even here tonight."

"He's like that all the time," Dennis says. "He's a weirdo. Hangs out with dogs more than he does people."

"My mind's a more interesting place than this is," I say with a grin. "And dogs provide much better company than the two of you." I allow myself to offer Chastity a wink at that and, to my relief, she smiles. Roddy, however, is not impressed.

"Don't even try it, *Sludge*," he warns, stepping over to Chastity and looping his arm around her waist. I appreciate his jealousy. Given that I don't even know his girlfriend—and he is, in fact, a far more attractive package than what I can currently offer—it's not much of a contest.

Roddy and Chastity take a few steps forward, and it's then that I realize why they stopped in the first place. We've reached the gate house for the coaster, the shack where people once loaded into the cars for their ride.

Dennis hops the old turnstile and steps onto the track. "We could totally walk this."

"What, out there?" Roddy looks along the track to where it stretches into the night beyond the shack.

"Roddy, that's *way* too dangerous," Chastity says.

"Nah, it's fine," Dennis says. "The track is solid. See?" He jumps a few times, and I'm sorely disappointed the track doesn't collapse under him.

Roddy doesn't look totally convinced. But his girlfriend gave him a perfectly reasonable warning, which means he is of course going to be a macho ass and ignore it.

"Coming, Dylan?" he asks as he steps away from Chastity's side. She gives him a wary glance, but she doesn't say anything else about what he's doing. Instead, she looks fearfully at me, like I might be stupid enough to join them.

"No way," I say. "Have fun. If you fall to your death, Dennis'll get his wish. Happy times for everyone."

Roddy rolls his eyes, and Dennis returns my earlier hand gesture before the two of them amble into the dark.

3

Chastity sighs and walks to the abandoned car that's still positioned on the track. She turns on her phone's flashlight and looks it over, her lips pursed in displeasure. Reaching a hand down, she wipes away some of the grime before climbing in and taking a seat on the car's far side.

"Want to join me?" she asks. "It's dry, at least."

Outside of the shack, my cousins are squealing like pigs because they think it's cool to taunt us with how thrilling their adventure is. I roll my eyes at their noises, hoping one of them slips and gets a mouthful of steel. A good bruise, maybe some lost teeth—then, at least, we could go back into town. The ER would be a sight better than this place. At least the hospital is warm.

Unless I'm blessed with witnessing such an accident, however, I don't think we're going to be returning home any time soon. So, I join Chastity in the old coaster car, wishing the damn thing had more to offer than its hard plastic seats.

"I hate being here," Chastity says after I've settled in beside her. She crosses her arms over her chest and sulks against the seatback.

"Me too," I say with a sardonic smile. "I got threatened with violence if I didn't partake. I sure as hell hope that wasn't the same with you."

She smiles. "No. Roddy didn't say where we were going. Or that we'd have company."

"Sorry we killed the romance," I say.

"Roddy killed the romance," she replies. "Roddy always kills the romance. Honestly, sometimes I don't even know why—"

"You like him?" I ask. She doesn't respond, and I shake my head. "Me neither." When I glance at her, I see the pinched irritation of someone who doesn't want my agreement. Furtively, I roll my eyes again before leaning forward and gripping the handrails on the seat front. "There's not always a rhyme or reason for it. People like who they like. It's just the way it goes."

"Yeah, but I *don't* like him," Chastity says. She gives a cute little snort that reminds me of Mim. "I guess that's the problem with small towns. Not a lot of choice, you know?"

"There's always a choice," I say. "Except for when there's not."

"Yeah, thanks kid. *Very* wise," she mutters.

She doesn't want me to agree with her, but she doesn't want my arguments, either. Apparently, I can't win, and I'm so cold and tired I really don't care. I pull down my hood and rake my fingers through the haphazard waves of my hair while, far-off, my idiot relatives yell obscenities into the night, their swears mixing with the steady drizzle of rain I can't believe hasn't already made one of them slip off the track.

Chastity listens to their antics with a huff. After a few minutes, she nudges my side. "I'm glad you stayed behind," she says. "I'd hate to be sitting here alone."

"Oh yeah, I'm *great* company," I mumble. I used to be good at this. At one point in my life, I could crack a smile on anyone—or make them want to deck me in the face. A fine line I loved to toe. But I don't have the energy anymore. Which makes me sound like sixty instead of sixteen. It's not that I've lost my zest. I've just gotten more selective about who gets to see it.

"I've had better," Chastity says. "But I've also had worse. At least I know you won't laugh at me."

I look at her. "Why would anyone laugh at you?"

She shrugs, suddenly uncomfortable. "I don't like this place. And, like, I know it's just empty because it lost too much money or whatever. Like, I know no one's died here. But, I don't know… it feels haunted, don't you think?" She looks at me, then presses her lips together. "Don't tell Roddy I said that. He'd make fun of me all night, trying to jump out and scare me or some other stupid shit."

"I won't tell him," I say. "But you don't have to worry. I'd know if this place was haunted."

I expect her to scoff and am surprised by the genuine interest that seeps into her expression instead.

"Seriously?" she asks. She lowers her voice, as if the others might overhear us. "Can you… do you…" she makes a rolling gesture with her hand, and I sit up straighter in the car's seat.

"Do you?" I ask. I've never come across another Sender in the wild. But then again, it's not really something you bring up in casual conversation.

Chastity, however, shakes her head. "No," she says with a smile. "But I believe. My grandmother. She could talk to the dead."

I study her profile, the shy way she turns her face from me as she divulges this truth. I don't know if her grandmother was a Sender or if she was just devoted to the idea of a spirit world, but either way it's obvious Chastity believed in her talents.

"I'm… attuned," I say after a minute. I don't really want to reveal my ability to a girl I don't know. Not with my cousins around. If the truth gets to them, I'll never hear the end of it. Besides, I can't see the type of ghosts this girl would be interested in. I've been around other Senders enough that I've got a better sense than most do when a place is haunted. But humans don't make themselves known to me, and I don't want anyone thinking I can contact Grandma from beyond the grave.

Even so, Chastity's smile widens, her soft features so pretty I wish this were a different situation. If we were here on a date, I'd stoop to some cheap tactics to try and win her affection with my ghostly know-how. But after tonight, I'll probably never see her again. And if I make a move on my cousin's girlfriend, I'll be the one visiting the ER.

Roddy screams something, a noise so loud it makes Chastity jump. She swears under her breath, then looks back at me.

"I'm sick of sitting here waiting for those two," she says. "Want to go for a walk? I know it's wet, but it beats looking like we can't move without them to guide us."

Her eyes widen in question, and I answer with a shrug of agreement. I hate sitting here too, and if we get far enough away from the bellows, maybe I can even convince Chastity to go down the paved hill at the front of the park so we can wait in Roddy's car. The idiot never locks up. We could curl up in the backseat, dry and slightly warmer while the other two wander around in the rain.

"Lead the way."

Chastity climbs out of the car on its far side. I follow, and together we slip out of the shack. As we head down the coaster's exit ramp on route to the rest of the park, I hunch into my coat and pull the hood back up to block some of the rain. We make it down a gravel slope and reach the wide, muddied path that leads into the park's main stretch.

As soon as my shoe squelches into the cold mud, I catch my first whiff of over-sweet stench.

"THIS PLACE WAS DONE UP LIKE AN OLD WESTERN TOWN," CHASTITY observes as we walk into the main part of the park, up the path and to the right where a street is laid out with old-fashioned store fronts lining each side.

"Yeah," I say as we approach the first store. I wipe my nose with a grimace. "I can still smell the leftover barbecue sauce."

Chastity eyes me sidelong. Then she grabs my sleeve and heads for the nearest building.

"Let's see if we can get inside," she says. "I'm already regretting this decision. The rain sucks. We've got to find somewhere else that's dry."

We slosh through puddles and I get a foot full of icy rainwater, the perfect torture to make my crappy night complete. With a groan, I hop up the porch on one foot and barrel unsteadily into the building, a whistle of wind accompanying my unbalanced strides. Inside, a fake chapel is lined with plain, wooden pews. I take a seat in the back row and pull off my sneaker so I can wring out my sock.

Chastity watches me with a look of wary distaste. "You shouldn't do that in here," she says.

"Why, you think this place is sacred?" I ask. I glance up at the front of the room, thinking about Mim and her quiet but fierce devotion. I could see her remonstrating me for dismissing a place even as fake as this one. The thought makes me smile.

"No," Chastity says as she drops into the pew across from me. "If you leave a wet spot on the floor, they'll know you were here."

"Who, the theme park police?" I sniff, the air in the chapel somehow colder than it was outside. Wet sock or no, my foot is freezing. I put the soaked fabric back on and squish it into my sopping shoe.

"I guess it doesn't matter," Chastity says, though she sounds unconvinced by her own words.

"No, it doesn't," I agree. "No one in their right mind would come here in December during a downpour in the middle of the night."

"We're here," she says.

I scoff. "I didn't come by choice. You didn't either. The other two… well, I stand by what I said. No one in their right mind would come here now."

Chastity laughs under her breath. She leans over and rests her arms on the pew in front of her. "I wonder what this place was like when it was open," she says. "What would the chapel have been used for, anyway? Surely they didn't have, like, actual services here."

"It was probably nothing but a resting place for tired old ladies who were sick of their walkers being dragged through the mud," I say. "That, or they held some fake shotgun weddings. Who knows? Maybe they held some real ones too."

"Shotgun ones?" Chastity snorts again. "That'd be an interesting sight."

"Can't have been too interesting," I say. I look around the room, unimpressed by its drab décor of white-washed walls and cheap red-velvet flooring. The pews are full of knicks, and the alter is nothing but a raised plywood dais. I crinkle my nose as I get another waft of sweet stench, and I swallow thick saliva, hugging my arms to my chest to try and stave off the cold.

"It's no wonder people didn't want to make the trek up the hill for this," I grumble. "So far, I've seen nothing worth the effort. And that'd be the truth even if it wasn't so miserable out."

"I can't argue with that," Chastity says. "It's pretty boring here, isn't it?"

"Yep." I nod, ruffling my hair before pulling my hood back up. "Which is why we should get the hell out of here. My foot's probably going to fall off from frost bite, and I can't get that awful smell out of my nose. Let's say we call it quits and go wait for the idiot twins down in the car. Let them frolic to their hearts' desires. I'm done with this place. The wind is starting to pick up, anyway. We don't want to get caught in a storm."

I drop my wet foot onto the ground and stand up. When I walk out into the aisle between the pews, Chastity looks up at me.

"What smell?" she asks.

I rub my nose. "What?"

"You keep talking about a smell," she says. "Old barbecue sauce? I don't smell anything."

"What do you mean, you don't—" I trail off, aware

of the wind kicking up another notch, despite the fact the building around us is not groaning with the impact of its push. I stare down at my hands, my gray palms balled into fists that shake with the cold. "Are you not frozen?" I ask.

Chastity shrugs her shoulders. "Yeah, I'm a bit chilly. But it's not *that* cold. Why… are you okay?"

She stands suddenly, as if she's afraid this is the onset of symptoms for my deadly disease. Which, to be fair, it kind of is. I'm not suffering from an illness, but I do have symptoms. It's just that this is the wrong sort of deadly.

I look at the chapel's door, then cross to it. The wind rises with each step, and the smell of rotted, sweet meat curdles under my nostrils as an icy shot stabs into my stomach and makes me wish I hadn't eaten a damn thing all day.

"Remember when you said this place seemed haunted?" I ask.

"Yeah," Chastity says from behind me. She sounds scared now. Scared of being here with me. Scared of being alone with the weird guy who's probably about to have some sort of fit.

"Remember when I told you I'd know if it was?" I continue. I step to the door and grip its handle.

"What are you talking about?" Chastity asks. She stands and walks to the far side of the pew, keeping her distance. "I-I think you're right. We should go. I'll find Roddy, and we'll leave. Okay?"

I should tell her she doesn't need to be afraid, let her know I'm not going to drop dead or try to turn her into a ghost myself. But right now, I've got other things on my mind. Things more important than this stranger's comfort.

"Why would I want to leave now?" I ask as I pull open the door and stagger back with the full force of the mammoth St. Bernard waiting on its other side. I catch my balance and move forward again, reaching a hand out to the ghost's cold, unsolid form. I look back at Chastity, and for the first time all night, I don't have to force my grin. "This place just got interesting."

Chastity is alarmed. I can't say I blame her. I've never seen my reflection while I'm next to a ghost. But these days, my normal appearance alarms people enough as it is. I doubt I'd make anyone's prize list in the looks department when a spirit's by my side. Back in the summer, I was told I've got some werewolf cosplay going on when the dead are nearby. Black circles around my yellow eyes and a wild glint that would put any stranger on edge. Poor Chastity probably thinks I'm about to keel over.

"We should get back," she says with a worried glance at the place where my hand touches the ghost's fur. It's a weird habit I know not many Senders share. I can't help it, though. For a lot of dogs, pets are a form of comfort, the kind of affection they've been longing for. Plus, it's a buzz I've never experienced anywhere else. The sensation of touching dead energy is something akin to sticking my hand in a radioactive spider's web, a tangled mass that is simultaneously frozen and lightning hot. As strange as it sounds, there is life to a ghost's matter. They are still beings comprised of energy, after all. Really, ghosts aren't actually dead. If they were, I wouldn't be able to see the hazy impression of a wagging tail as I stroke this St. Bernard.

My first summer at Camp Wanagi I wrote a paper about zombie movies, reckoning that the undead were close enough to what we experience to be lumped under the same broad definition. This dog is not a zombie. But I *would* classify her as a creature undead. She's not alive, but she's not inactive matter rotting in the ground. The flesh may be gone. But the spirit lives. And it wants my attention.

I may not be up for middle of the night thrill seeking and family bonding. But I am always happy to help a dog in need.

"You don't have to be afraid," I tell Chastity. I try not to make it obvious how queasy my stomach is as I speak. "I'm fine. And I'm not about to, you know, try to maim you or anything… just in case that's your concern."

I glance to the right side of the chapel where she's standing and see that I've managed to get a small smile out of her. She follows the line of my arm to where my hand rests over what to her must look like nothing but air.

"What do you see?" she asks, her voice timid but— thankfully—not mocking.

"A ghost," I answer with as little pomp as possible. I don't want to make it too theatrical an experience. Not for an outsider on her first sighting.

Chastity pulls her long hair back, giving me flashes of

Korni as she tilts her head and nods towards my hand.

"What are you doing?" she asks. Not 'are you crazy?' or 'are you sure you're not having an episode?' It's a nice question, plain and simple. So, I give her a nice response.

"Petting her," I say, then laugh as Chastity's face scrunches up in confusion. "Sorry, didn't I mention? It's a canine ghost. A St. Bernard." I turn back to the dog, my head full of the whooshing wind that comes whenever a ghost is near. "Can't fathom what the hell she's doing out here, though."

My own thought spoken aloud is enough of a prompt. The dog barks, a low roar of a woof that makes me wince. Then she bounds off down the park's main street, and I bolt into the rain, afraid she'll get too far ahead.

"Where are you going?" Chastity calls, her voice separate from the wind as if the two sounds enter my head by way of different ears.

"After her!" I yell back.

I feel bad leaving Chastity alone in the cold, rainy dark, but the dog's welfare ranks higher on my list of priorities. This isn't a locale I can visit multiple times until I've slowly puzzled out the dog's unfinished business. I've only got one shot at this, unless I make a plea for the Oracle to get involved. But nice and simple is the better way to go. I've got to do my best to solve this tonight, if I can.

Not that I need to feel bad, anyway. After half a minute of running, I hear splashing footsteps behind me as Chastity tries to catch up. She'll have a hard time running at my speed, but I'm impressed she's willing to try. It'd be easy for her to head back to the coaster where her boyfriend has got to be tiring of walking aimlessly along the track. Going further into the park after the freak who chases dead dogs means this girl is something special.

The dog runs down the main street and then off to the side, past the smaller rides and in through the wall of another building. I rush to the door, pulling and swearing when it snags. Chastity catches up to me while I'm still trying to pry it open.

"It's not locked," I say as she comes to a heaving stop at my side. "It's just stuck."

"Why are you trying to get in here?" she asks. She studies my face for a few seconds, then nods before I've offered up any response. "Ghost. Right. Okay, stand aside Little Man."

I step back with an indignant scoff, and Chastity smirks as she grips the door handle. She wrenches it open in one easy pull.

"All right, that was impressive," I admit. "Heightism aside."

She laughs. "I didn't discriminate against you for being short," she argues. "I just stated it as fact."

"Yeah, 'cause I was under the grand illusion I was six foot five," I mutter.

"What's worse—Little Man or Sludge?" she asks.

"It's a toss-up," I say as I peer into the building. I can't see the dog, but I still sense and smell her. "I'd take 'Dylan' over both, all things considered equal."

"Noted," Chastity says. "So long as you promise that if our paths cross after this night, you will never, ever call me *babe*."

I laugh as I step into the dark building. "You've got a deal. Now let's find our ghost."

THE BUILDING WE RUSH INTO DOESN'T HAVE THE SAME WESTERN FLARE of the park's main road. Instead, it looks to be laid out like a makeshift performance hall. The space isn't large, but there are rows of benches and a stage shrouded in darkness at the hall's far end.

Rain drops onto the roof and wind rushes in my head as I search for the dog. I don't see another exit in plain view, which means the ghost either ran straight through the middle of the building, or else I need to go farther inside.

"This place is creepy," Chastity says beside me. "It feels more like a spook house than a stage."

I wave a dismissive hand. "You only think that because you know we're ghost-hunting. Before, the place was empty. Now, it's not."

"Maybe," Chastity says. She stays by my side and grabs her phone to turn on the flashlight. I glance at her battery and see it's sitting at around twenty-five percent.

"Save that," I say with a nod at the phone. "She'll drain it if you're not careful. We might have to call someone if we get… in a situation."

"Situation?" Chastity stops while I cross the hall and climb onto the stage. "What sort of situation?"

"With a ghost? You never can tell," I say. "Hey, what's this?"

In front of me, right in the middle of the stage, is a half-wall. I reach out to it as I climb, wanting to use it to steady my balance. But as soon as I grab hold, the whole wall starts to twist.

"Must be on a track," Chastity says. She joins me on the stage and pushes against the wall. "Yeah, see? If you turn it, it spins and—holy crow, what the frig is that?"

She jumps back, and I turn, half-expecting to see the dog. But it's not a ghost meeting my gaze. It's a pair of large, cartoonish eyes.

"Damn, that's disturbing," I say. I step forward onto the moving platform and approach what I assume was once an animatronic animal seated before a player piano. "Never mind, I take back what I said. This place is *way* creepier than the chapel."

"Uh-huh," Chastity agrees. "It's so weird that all of this was just left here. Why not take the pieces away? Why not sell them?"

"Do you know anyone who would want a creepy animatronic piano playing cat—or whatever the hell this is supposed to be?" I ask.

She shrugs. "Someone would. People are weird."

A bloom of rotted meat reminds me of the dog I'm supposed to be following, and I turn my back on the performer. "Tell me about it," I say as I head deeper into the dark folds of the stage. I cross by other animatronic animals, a whole gang set up to play some pre-recorded song. I wonder if it ever sounded good, or if even in the park's prime this stage show was a nightmare of off-tune notes and mechanical creaks from beneath the fake, tattered fur. It's a good thing I'm not here with anyone who could make those things swing. I like the fact that my talent as a Sender does not include being attacked by ghosts or witnessing inanimate objects brought to terrifying life.

I climb over another revolving platform and push past an old costume trunk that's split open and spilling fabric. Chastity stays on my heels as I pick through the remnants of the production, peering around my shoulder to try and get a look at what's ahead of us.

"So, what's it like seeing ghosts?" she asks as we pass a nook full of sound equipment that's still hooked up, ready to play.

Her tone is so conversational it makes me laugh. "It's… interesting," I say.

"Is everyone a ghost? Or is it really only those with unfinished business?" she asks.

"It doesn't work exactly like that," I say. "Unfinished business is not so easy to define. Some ghosts have a clear motive for staying. Others… not so much." My gaze cuts to the left so I can see her head where it hovers above my shoulder. "I don't see the kinds of ghosts you think I see," I add.

"What's that supposed to mean?" she asks, and I don't fail to notice the defensive edge to her words. "How many types of ghosts are there?"

"As many as there are species of life, I guess." I pause and sigh, half-turning to face her. "I can't talk with your grandmother."

Chastity halts, stunned that I've picked out the question she didn't want to actually ask. It was a guess, but not a total shot in the dark. The few non-Senders in my life who have semi-believed in my abilities always want to know if I can communicate with some lost relative or tragically fated childhood friend.

"My grandmother didn't have unfinished business," she says in a sulkier tone, an 'I didn't want that, anyway' kind of suggestion.

I roll my eyes and turn back to the task at hand. "I see the ghosts of dogs," I say. "Not people." I walk a few steps and then stop at the stage's back wall. "Damn it, there's nowhere else to go."

"So, what's that like, then?" Chastity asks. "Seeing the ghosts of dogs? And don't say *interesting*. I'm not an idiot, you know."

"I know," I say as my gaze travels the length of the wall, looking for a hidden door I missed on my first glance. "Seeing dogs is great. I like being able to help them. But it's not a pleasant off-leash walk, so to speak. For a long time, I didn't know how to communicate with them. So I just… saw them. And I couldn't do anything about it. That sucked. But I love dogs, so it's always been kind of cool."

"I've never met someone who can see ghost dogs before," Chastity says. "Are there a lot of you?"

"Not that I know of," I say with a shrug. "I'm weird. I guess we all are, aren't we? Whether you see ghosts or not, all of us are freaks in our own special way. But my friends—the ones who also, you know—they see humans. I've never met anyone else who sees dogs."

"You're unique, even among the unique," Chastity says.

I shrug. "Suppose so. Lucky me, huh? Crazy talents *and* astounding good looks." I flash her my widest grin, and she laughs. Then I turn away before the laugh drops into a more pitying smile. "The dog must have gone through the wall, after all," I say. "We'll have to turn back and try going around the building's side."

I spin on my heel to start the walk back to the main entrance. But as I brush by Chastity, she grabs my arm.

"Wait." She points to the wall, near the far corner. When I stop, I hear a soft scraping through the wind in my head. "Is that a hole?"

I look at where she's pointing, then approach it to get a better view. In the farthest corner of the stage, a bit of the wall has been cut. A circle that's possibly wide enough to squeeze through heads out behind the performance hall. When I push away the remnants of the wall's siding, I see blue-white wisps waiting on the other side.

"Well, nothing for it," I say with another sigh. "Looks like we're going down on all fours."

7

THE SQUEEZE THROUGH THE HOLE IS TIGHT. I MANAGE TO SQUIRM THROUGH okay after taking off my jacket and pushing it ahead of me. But Chastity gets stuck.

"You should have stayed back on the main strip," I complain. The dog is waiting, patient because, well… she's dead, and I'm probably the first living thing to ever see her. But she's relying on me, and I hate that I'm wasting time trying to pry loose a near-stranger's belt loop from where it's snagged on some siding.

"Thanks, jackass," Chastity mutters. She fishes something from her pocket. Keys and, looped in with them, a knife. "Use this."

I take the knife and slice through one end of the belt loop. Then I grab Chastity's arms and haul her the rest of the way through the hole.

When she gets up onto her feet again, she doesn't thank me for my assistance. Instead, she raises a brow in dubious consideration of my chest. "What the hell are you wearing?"

I threw my coat back on as soon as I was out of the building. But I haven't yet zipped it up, which means Chastity now has a good view of the purple pajama shirt covered in Weiner dogs that my stupid sisters bought as a joke but which—joke's on them—is ridiculously comfortable.

"Everyone is a fashion critic," I say, zipping up my coat and refusing to defend my choices to someone I don't even know. "Come on. We've got to get moving. No more fooling around."

"Yeah, because that was a barrel of laughs," Chastity mutters. She surveys the area. "Where are we?"

It's a fair question. We've exited the building, but the landscape around us now is tangled woods instead of the wide, muddied path that led us from the coaster to the main strip and over to the performance hall. The walk through the dark stage must have brought us around a weird curve veering away from the path. Now that we've shimmied under the back wall, we're treading through the wilds beyond the park grounds.

"I don't know." I shrug, then give the dog a pat to let her know she's got my attention. I expect her to keep moving, but she doesn't. She sits—as well as a ghost dog *can* sit—while the shady spots of her eyes stay fixed on me. For a ghost who doesn't actually have a stare, her gaze is unnerving. Intense. I crouch down, the wind kicking up in my head and my whole body wrapping in ice. Hugging myself for warmth, I lower until I'm eye level with the dog.

"What are you—" Chastity begins, but I hold up a hand to stop her talking.

"This is the part where I become an even bigger

jackass," I say. "I need you to be quiet. Absolutely quiet, okay? It's important."

I'm poised to hear grumbling or an all-out telling off by the girl who's had enough of this terrible adventure. But Chastity does not make a sound. She finds a nearby tree and leans against it, waiting. I flick my eyes up to her and give her an approving nod. Then I look back at the dog.

Cal made fun of me in the summer for trying to communicate with ghost dogs, but being able to do it is by far the coolest thing I've ever experienced. It's not like talking to them. Not like hearing thoughts or seeing images in my mind. It's just... ideas. Vague impressions that barely even register *as* ideas until they slowly curl together and form into something my brain is able to comprehend. It's kind of like cotton candy. A bunch of sugary grains that start spinning, and somehow or other they end up melting and stretching and connecting together, until lo and behold a whole cone of artificial amazingness exists.

I could go for some cotton candy right now. Despite the meal I gorged on earlier tonight, I'm suddenly aching with hunger. Except, I'm not really. My stomach is queasy, and I don't think cotton candy or anything else would go down very well. But the hunger remains. The idea of hunger. An idea that's not my own.

Hunger. That's what the dog died of. I understand that quick enough, and my heart aches for this big girl and her pain. The hunger killed her. But it's not what made her stay. Something else. Something here, in this park. Something close.

"Show me," I say. Her ears are not well-formed, only smoky impressions in the night. But still, I notice how they perk at my words. She hears me, and she understands. I give her another pat before stretching my wobbly legs and rising to my full height. The dog stands as well, moving at a slower, more careful pace.

Somewhere in the distance, my cousins yell. I hear them calling Chasity's name, no doubt wondering where the hell the two of us went. I follow behind the dog and glance back at the living girl still leaning against the tree.

"You can come, if you'd like," I tell her. "Or you can leave. It's up to you."

She stares at the back of the performance hall, mulling her options. "Where are you going?" she asks.

"To see why this ghost is still around," I reply.

The response is simple. But it's enough. As soon as I continue off behind the dog, Chastity pushes away from the tree and steps to my side.

THE GROWTH GETS THICK AS SOON AS WE'RE A LITTLE WAYS OFF FROM THE performance hall. I step between trees, thankful the branches at least offer some mild protection from the rain. Not that it matters much at this point. I'm soaked, frozen, and sick. By the time this night is over, I might very well be as ill as my mother and step-mother think I am. They'll fly me home and check me into the hospital, probably. I'll spend the rest of Hanukkah in a sick bed, alone and bored out of my mind.

But if I get this dog released before that happens, it'll be well worth the inconvenience.

"Do I still need to be quiet?" Chastity asks as we weave between bushes and brambles.

"Not at this particular moment," I say. The way forward would be easy enough if this were the daytime. But it's pitch black within the tangle of trees, and what rain still gets through makes the ground slippery.

"Good," Chastity says. "You looked freaky back

there. You know? You're all sorts of freaky."

"I know," I say. "It's pretty cool, huh?"

Chastity laughs. "Yeah. It kind of is. But what are you doing now? What was all of that crouching and staring about?"

"We were having a chat," I say. "And now she's showing me why she's still here."

"That's incredible." The compliment is genuine, and I'm tempted to tell her she's the incredible one. I've never met someone who believed in my talent as quickly as she has. Given her apparent inability to recognize just how much of a loser my cousin is, I can't totally disregard the possibility that Chastity is a bit gullible. But I don't think she's stupid. Trusting, maybe. But not so trusting she'd believe someone was seeing ghosts without having a good reason for it.

I continue along the soft ground until my foot hits something hard. Confused, I pause and bend low to look at what I'm standing on. It takes a moment before I realize it's a coaster track. Glancing up, I peer through the dark trees ahead of us, wondering if we've somehow twisted back to the coaster at the edge of the park. But the big looping track is nowhere to be seen. This must be a second, smaller coaster—one that is so forgotten it's become a part of the wilderness.

"Looks like we'll be daring idiots, after all," I say. I step onto the track, glad it's level with the forest floor. "She's taking us along a coaster."

The metal of the track is disguised for the first while, so covered with mud and leaves it's indistinguishable from the earth. But a little ways on, it raises slightly, and the metal becomes hollow beneath our feet as we pick carefully along.

"Why does Roddy think this is fun?" Chastity asks when her foot slips and she crashes into my back. "This is horrible. And we're at least close to the ground."

"He probably thinks he's some deep soul who experiences life to the utmost," I mutter. The dog is getting further ahead, so I try to hurry my pace. "I get it—sort of. I used to kind of think the same. But then I got a second-hand account of how shitty being a ghost is, and it occurred to me that dying young because I was intentionally stupid would probably end with me being a tormented soul. I don't know… maybe some people really feel at one with the universe when they do stuff like that. But Roddy? He's just trying to show off because he thinks it makes him cool."

"You're right," Chastity sighs. "And the worst part is, it works. He *is* cool. How sad is that?"

"Intensely," I say. I glance over my shoulder with a grin. "Being cool is very overrated."

Chastity smiles and nudges me forward, but when I turn back I don't move. The rotted meat is still in my nose, and the wind is rushing all around me. But the dog has disappeared.

"What is it?" Chastity asks when she realizes I'm remaining still.

"She must have gotten ahead of us," I mumble.

I take a step to where the track once more starts to tangle with the underbrush. The dog must have continued on, past the coaster and into the woods. I make another search for her, then move forward. But when I do, the ground beneath me proves to be unsolid, and I land back on my ass as one foot drops into open space below.

"Help me up," I groan. Chastity doesn't hesitate.

Grabbing my waist, she hauls me to my feet and holds me steady while I pull free my foot. "There's something under here."

"What sort of something?" Chastity asks. She sounds wary again, staying behind me as I take a shuffling step closer to where I pierced through the mud.

"Only one way to find out," I say. I stand at the edge of the coaster track and bring one foot up. Then I stomp down hard on the soft portion of the ground.

And realize too late that my footing was inaccurate. I wasn't standing on the edge of the track. I was between slats, and with my eager push, the whole tangle of brush falls away—bringing Chastity and me with it.

"OH, HELL NO," CHASTITY MOANS FROM SOMEWHERE ON TOP OF ME. I CAN'T see anything, and the smell of rotted meat is so strong I can't properly breathe. Of course, my respiratory distress could also have something to do with the girl collapsed over my back. Hard to say for sure.

"If at all possible…" I struggle, my face uncomfortably close to the dirt. "Could you please get off of me?"

"I'm trying," Chastity says. She grunts, casting off some loose twigs and then rolling to my left. The lack of her weight gives me a bit more wiggle room. But even without her pressing me into the dirt, I still have trouble breathing through the scent.

"It's close," I say as I push up to my knees. "Whatever she wants to show me. It's close now."

"No kidding," Chastity says. She coughs. "You've got some nose on you if you smelled this all the way back on the strip."

My head twists to see her better. She holds a hand to her mouth, her whole face scrunched up like she's trying hard not to gag.

"You can smell it?" I ask.

"I can smell something," she mutters. "Oh, it's awful!"

"It is that," I say. I watch her for a few more seconds before I check out the rest of our surroundings. Digging my keys out of my pocket, I push on the travel light I keep close for emergencies. It's a solid little thing with a battery that holds up better than the one on my phone. I shine it around the burrow we've found ourselves in.

"It's like a tunnel," Chastity says. She glances up, back to the surface. We haven't fallen far, and we've more slid downwards than actually fallen, anyway. It's a well-hidden slope curving down to a sheltered area in the undergrowth. It's something that wouldn't be out of place in the woods. But this isn't the woods. Not really. This is a bit of woodland on the edges of an abandoned amusement park.

Safe. It's a safe place, hidden from… from what? From view? No. From the elements. The rain only dribbles down at the edge of the slope. Farther into this makeshift tunnel, we're relatively dry—or we would be, if we weren't soaked prior to our unexpected visit. It's a good place for a dog to shelter overnight. But why here? What the hell was a St. Bernard ever doing in a place like this?

With my thoughts of her, the ghost reappears. I lower the light as I take in the sight of her bulky mass, the wisps so wide they are barely contained in this small space.

"What were you doing here, girl?" I ask.

I reach out to pet her misty coat. Touching her is a little like getting static shocks through my fingertips. Cold, but jolting. Surprising, every time.

"Maybe she belonged to one of the park owners," Chastity offers. The suggestion is a sound one. But it's not correct. I know it's not.

"She didn't," I say with a shake of my head. I stare at the dog, pat her shocking coat. "She... she was traveling."

"Traveling?" Chastity says. "Up here?"

"Yes. Yes she was," I say. "But then..." I lift my chin and look past the ghost. Raising the light, I shine it deeper into the tunnel. I can't fully stand, but I can wriggle forward on my knees. I do, until I can make out the heap of rotting flesh that once belonged to the enormous canine.

I lower my head, sick and hurting.

"She's here," I say. "Her body's here. She must have gotten stuck, and that's why—"

The dog barks in my head. She's been fairly quiet, but now she barks, again and again. Louder and louder. I force myself to look at her remains, trying to understand what she wants me to discover. But it's not her carcass that's problematic. It's the feeling in my gut. An odd, unsettled feeling I can't place. A cold, dead feeling that's almost as if...

"I think there's another ghost," I say. The dog barks again, and I groan against the sudden rush of wind in my head.

"Another dog?" Chastity asks.

"I can't see it," I say. "But I think... It must be a person. Must..."

Where the hell are my friends when I need them?

This would be easy with Korni by my side. I don't like the guy, but even Meander would be useful right now—he'd probably get us killed in the process, but at least I'd know what I was facing before I died. I can't see human ghosts. I don't even know if there *is* one now. There's just this feeling, like the dog is suddenly more than itself. Like there's something else present.

Dogs don't always wander alone. They are pack animals. They like to be with family. Whatever form that family takes.

"Of course," I say. I glance back at the dog, and she barks a final time. Then I hold my hand over my mouth and carefully approach the St. Bernard's corpse. I shine the light over it—beyond it. I hold it up until I can see the second corpse, the one bundled in coats and with a backpack shoved up against its side.

My vision tilts, and I slump against the side of the tunnel. Pulling my knees up, I tuck my head between them and let out a low groan.

"Chastity," I say in a weak voice, "how's that battery of yours doing?"

I listen as she fumbles for her phone. "Fifteen percent. Why?"

"You might want to make a phone call," I say from between my knees. "The police need to know we've found a body."

RODDY'S NOT HAPPY. WHEN THE FIRST SIRENS FLASH UP THE SIDE OF THE hill, we hear him screaming for Chastity, ready to bolt away to the safety of his car. We don't stay in the burrow, so we wind up meeting my cousins on the main strip of the park.

"Why are the cops here?" Roddy says as soon as he spots us, although I don't think he suspects it's us who's called them. "They couldn't have seen us. They wouldn't know…"

"Geez, Roddy," Chastity says. "You think a whole fleet of cars is going to show up to shoo off some trespassing teenagers? Get a grip."

She's soaked through and covered with mud. There's even a leaf stuck in behind her ear. And she's freaking beautiful. I want to grab her hand, but I don't push my luck. I tug on her arm instead and we wait by the park gates for the police to get out of their cars. They're not happy, either, but that doesn't matter once we show them what we've found. It's funny how perspectives shift. Trespassing in the park is a major offence. But after stumbling across the body of a drifter who thought it'd be fun to explore and wound up falling into the burrow and getting himself killed, we were suddenly more heroes than hooligans.

Dennis goes pale when he figures out why the police are really here. Roddy goes pale when he realizes that the two of them were one misstep away from sharing the drifter's fate. I go gray—grayer—as soon as I'm back by the ghost. *Ghosts,* I think. I can't be certain, but the full feeling is there when we get back to the burrow. Like there is too much energy for such a small space. Like there's something else taking up all the remaining room in my head.

The police cordon off the area, ask us a million questions, and then send us to wait in the back of the cop cars. Roddy tries to get his girlfriend by his side, but Chastity sits with me, leaving him and Dennis to share the backseat of another cruiser. I watch through the rainy window as they at last remove the drifter's body. Then I scramble out of the car to go and badger them until someone assures me they're bringing along the St. Bernard as well.

The ghost of the dog follows her body. When it's loaded into a van, she wags her misty tail and looks at me long enough to issue a final, dizzying bark. Then she sits next to someone I can't see. Her head tilts up, and the smoke around her ears dips in a way I know means the drifter is patting her head. I've never seen two ghosts interacting before. I've never felt so awful and amazing at the same freaking time.

"You really must have seen something," Chastity

mumbles. She crawls out of the car and steps behind me, while my eyes stay fixed on the dog's brightening glow.

"You didn't actually believe me?" I ask.

"I don't know," Chastity says. "Sort of did. Sort of thought you were crazy."

"And now?"

She laughs. "You're a little of both?"

I can feel the change coming, hear how the wind is softening in my head, see the hazy glow as it settles into something strong and light. The energy is shifting, and it would be okay, if I were here with a bunch of Senders. But I've discovered something in my time alone. Those who can't connect can't share. Non-Senders don't expel the same energy us chosen ones do. And if there are two ghosts—even if I can only see one of them—this release is going to be big.

"Just do me a favor," I say to Chastity. "Well, two favors, actually."

"What?" Chastity asks.

I step back, close to where she stands. "After all of this is over, try to remember me as the mysterious stranger who solved a paranormal investigation, okay?"

"Okay." She laughs again. "And the other favor?"

I sigh, hoping her reflexes are fast. Hoping she'll break my fall before I hit the gravel lot.

"Catch," I mumble. And then it all goes black.

KORNELÍA

haze outside the car's window. I stare at the brightness as it streams past in the opposite direction, wishing we were heading that way too. Back to our home. Back to our tree, with its glowing lights and prickles of sappy green. Bruno is probably asleep on the sofa next to it, tired from waking so early to check his shoe. Tonight, he's expecting noisy Hurðaskellir and hoping for another gift once morning arrives. My baby brother is diligent when it comes to observing our most cherished Yuletide traditions, and he is particularly overjoyed whenever one of the older kids is gifted not candy or toys, but a potato—their punishment for not finishing their dinners or for refusing to help our father in the barn. Most of the time, Bruno is a wild a bundle of excitement, always yearning for a new adventure. But in December, he is the best behaved of us all.

I am not at home with my baby brother, however.

I am in a car with the eldest of our clan, a quiet car which persists in taking us further from the yellow-white lights of our sharp-scented tree. Kristján doesn't listen to music when he drives in the fog. He's too worried about veering off the road into a rolling green field. The weather is not to his liking. But this is the only day we were able to sneak away from the farm. He needs to take some photos, and he wants to take them on the beach. He wouldn't miss this chance, no matter how uncomfortable the drive makes him.

"We'll be there soon," he says as we curve into a bend in the road.

"Good," I reply. I don't mean to be such an active participant in the silence, but we've been driving for hours—and these days, I'm not good at idle conversation. On long drives or long treks on foot, I used to make a game of remarking on the things I saw around me. The colors of the landscape. The position of the clouds in the sky. The quality of whatever few cars traveled by on the lonely road. But I can't comment on those things anymore. I can't see them well enough to offer any opinion on their shapes and hues. Today, all I see are vague impressions of the interior of our car and glinting lights from the vehicles we pass. I can make out spots of greenery beyond the window, but I can no longer discern what that greenery is. I can't even tell that it's foggy outside. Not with my eyes. I only know that because of the careful way Kristján drives.

"We won't take long," he says as the car turns again. "I just have a few shots to get for my portfolio." He pauses, and I can feel his gaze on me. He's nervous about mentioning anything to do with his application to the arts academy in the Netherlands. He thinks

I'll feel like he's abandoning me if we talk about his leaving home.

"We'll get some great shots," I assure him. I reach my hand out, fumble for where his is somewhere near the center console. When I find it, I give it a squeeze. "You're talented, Kristján. You'll be a great photographer."

"Mom and Dad will have a fit if I get in," he says. He squeezes my hand back, a little too tightly. "I doubt I will, anyway."

He will get in. I know enough of my brother's work to be positive his acceptance is forthcoming. And despite his self-scrutiny, excitement hovers behind his every thought, jumping each time he imagines opening the welcome package they will send to our door. He's worked out all the details of how he'll live, knows already which courses he wants to take. He's saved some money, is fighting for scholarships, and he is already fluent in Dutch, which will serve him well in trying to obtain part-time work once he's abroad. I will miss him when he moves, but I would never begrudge him his success. I'm sad he doesn't quite believe that—disappointed he thinks his poor, sight-impaired sister will resent his leaving her behind.

I've always existed behind others. The concept is not a new one for me. I'm forever behind in my studies at school. Behind in understanding my place at home. Even behind in developing my talents as a Sender, although that delay was always the easiest to bear. I still remember what it was like to receive my first invitation to Camp Wanagi. I remember the fight my parents had about whether they would let me go, all while I sat on the stairs and listened in secret, hoping they would because it felt like—for the first time in my life—I was getting ahead. When I arrived at camp, I realized that my abilities were not as impressive as everyone else's. But being behind in the Oracle of Senders still meant I was ahead of the quiet, monotonous life I had always expected for myself at home.

I know my brother will feel the same when his acceptance package arrives. Kristján's chance for achievement will come with his welcome to the arts academy. I want him to seize it, because I know how fleeting it can be.

I was so looking forward to my birthday last month, when my talents would finally blossom and I could understand the truth of my role as a Sender. If I wasn't going to get ahead, I at least looked forward to catching up with the other Shades. But all turning sixteen gave me was another strike to my sight, and a new drum of periodic headaches to go with it. I haven't seen any spirits in the past month. I've been stuck in our house, too clumsy and stumbling to venture anywhere without a sibling to help guide me back to more familiar quarters.

We all have a beginning and an end. What happens in between is a shuffling of successes and failures as we strive to keep some semblance of balance and, if ever possible, tilt the scales in a favorable way. My brother has never understood why I like going to a camp for people who see the dead. But I have always been more content among spirits because they help me understand the balance—help me strive to achieve it. They let me see that even amongst the failures of my life, there can be successes as well.

I hope I see another ghost soon. Because I don't

mean to complain. I never used to, much. But it's been hard, becoming so frail. So dependent on others. So helpless. So useless.

I never want my brother to feel like I do now.

"We're here," Kristján says. His hand drops from mine as he turns the steering wheel. We slow and stop, and he shifts into park before switching off the ignition. I listen to the dinging of the open door, readjusting the frames of my glasses as I stare out the blurry window and wait for him to help me out of the car.

I SMELL THE OCEAN WELL BEFORE I CAN MAKE OUT THE RHYTHMIC SHADOW of its lapping tide. Salt mixes with the fog as Kristján walks with me down to the beach. We are the only ones out here. It's cold, and the weather is not pleasant. But it is a photographer's dream.

Kristján stops not far from the water's edge. "Let me get my camera set up," he says. "Then we'll start."

I wait, listening to the clicks and snaps of his work, the sound of the water rushing in and out of my left ear. The world around me is dim, dark and gray. It's beautiful, even if I can't fully appreciate the beauty with my eyes. I've been here before, and I know well what this place looks like. I tilt my head towards the shoreline, the air sharp and stinging against my skin. I love the cold freshness of open places like this. Perhaps I was remiss in wishing I could be at home just now. This place is not as familiar as the farm. But compared to the warm stuffiness of our house, the black beach feels a little like freedom.

"Okay, I'm ready, Kornelía," Kristján says. "All I want is for you to walk. Just take a slow walk down the beach, in a straight line."

He pauses, unease rolling off him like the waves by our side as he wonders if I'll be okay to traverse this uneven terrain by myself.

"The ocean is to my left," I tell him. "I can see enough to know where I'm going, Kristján. I'll be fine."

"Okay." I hear his intake of breath as he steps forward and combs down the back of my hair. "You can start walking now."

I do walk, the shuddering clicks of his camera fading as the space between us grows. My brother insisted I be the model for his photos. He said I looked the best in this surreal place, although I don't understand why. I am clumsy, too stickly and long for my own good. But he says I have a *look* about me—as if that means anything. After all, whatever his vision, he's only interested in capturing it via the back of my head.

The walk is peaceful, at least. I don't have to worry about bumping into chairs or stepping on scattered toys when I'm out here. My legs extend in blurry blue, my jeans fading into boots that are close enough to the shade of the sand that I cannot easily distinguish my feet from the ground. When I look down, it's as if my feet are disappearing in the blackness under me. Gray above and black below. Gray-brown stone to my right and gray-blue water to my left. The palate is dull and uninviting. Yet very few would view this place with disinterest.

I miss these moments of calm. I used to have them often, sketching in my room or outside by the barn.

Sometimes, Kristján and I would hike through the fields and dip our toes in a heated spring as we both worked on our own art. I miss drawing. The last time I picked up a pencil was on the first day of November. I drew a woman, one I'd sensed years ago but who I suddenly realized I'd never drawn. The likeness, when I finished, was horrid. She looked nothing like how I envisioned her in my head. I threw the pencil away, irritated by my own waning talent. A week later, my vision blurred more, and I couldn't even make out the lines when I tried to study the picture anew.

I miss being able to see with clarity. I miss being able to draw with precision. I miss being around the dead, where I at least still feel like my presence can be of some use.

"All right, Kornelía!" Kristján calls. He jogs towards me, and I turn back to see the thick shape of him approaching like a life-sized teddy bear clad all in brown. "I think that's good," he says when he reaches my side. "I'll take some of you sitting next."

He directs me to a spread of black sand, and I sit where he asks. I wish I could see more of the ocean view before me, but the cold, the breeze, and the sound of the rushing water are enough to keep me complacent. Crisp memories of my past visits transpose over the blurred landscape my weak eyes now offer. It's not quite the same. But it's good enough.

Kristján snaps photos, and I smile when he curses after getting down onto the sand before realizing it's wet. When he helps me up, I wipe at the dampness of my jeans where I was sitting, watching as my brother goes through the photographs and wishing so much that I could go through them with him.

"Get anything decent?" I ask. "I mean, you always get something decent. Any better than decent today?"

"A few," Kristján says, and I can hear the smile in his voice even if I can't quite make out the curve of it on his face. "One really excellent one. You make a wonderful model." I shake my head, and he laughs. "You do! Can you imagine Sigrid here? She would do nothing but pull faces every time I tried to click."

Kristján is the oldest of seven, followed by me. My sister Sigrid comes next, and my big brother is right about her lack of cooperation. She and Bruno are cut from the same cloth. Both wild and vibrant and beautiful. But not exactly a tonal fit for what Kristján wants to capture today.

If nothing else, I'm glad that I have been useful to my brother. I used to do a lot around our farm, caring for the little ones and tending to the animals. I like being valuable to Kristján now. As little as my help is, my participation in this photoshoot has made him smile.

"There are some rocks over there where we can sit," Kristján says. "Let's stop for a break. It's cold out here. Want some coffee?"

"Yes, I'd love some," I say.

My brother holds out his arm, and I take it, the ocean lapping behind my head and my fuzzy vision slipping from side to side as we move to the rocks. I like the cold. But this beach is so quiet and bare that it's starting to make me dizzy. A warm beverage will help to ground me. Warmth in my hands and cold all around will help solidify my placement in this strange, foggy world.

"Applications are due in February," Kristján says. He scans through his photos, inspecting each one for flaws. Insecurity wavers through him as he considers the shots, worries of his own worth cycling in my head almost as if the emotions are mine instead of his. "If I get the portfolio completed by the end of the month, I'll have time to work on everything else." He drops the camera into my hand, a force of habit he doesn't at first notice. "Which one do you think—"

He stops, his question dying away as he tries to backpedal and remove the camera from my grasp. I grip its sides, holding it firm as I stare at the blurry screen and feel my way across the commands until I reach the button to move between photographs.

"The second one," I say with a smile. I turn my face to my brother and laugh. "It's always the second one with you."

Kristján laughs too, trying to hide the fearful ache

in his gut by forcing a mirthful bellow. I hand back the camera and pick up the flask of coffee from the rock beside me. Then I take a sip, ignoring the tapping pulse of pain starting at the edge of my temple as I push hair behind my ears.

"Stop feeling guilty," I say as I stare out at the water. "It's not your fault I'm losing my sight."

"I—" Kirstján falters, unsure of what to say. My brother's never been much of a wordsmith. But for sixteen years that hasn't mattered. The two of us have always communicated through images. His photos and my drawings. Suddenly, it's as if we've lost the ability to speak to each other. "Are you sure you don't mind if I take the camera to school with me?"

I laugh again, this time more genuinely. "Why would I mind?"

"Well, it's *our* camera," he says. Technically, this is true. But only technically. My brother and I pooled our money, diving into our respective stashes of cash gifts and funds collected on long summer days when the neighboring farms needed extra help. I told him I wanted to try my hand at photography—that we could share the equipment and the hobby. But I only said that because he wouldn't accept my money outright.

Kristján has never left Iceland, but his photographs will allow him to. We both love our home and our family. But sometimes it feels like we are meant to offer the world something greater in exchange for its letting us exist. Kristján captures the beauty of this planet through his photographs, displaying it and promoting it so others might learn to appreciate it as well. And I—I help the dead.

Or I used to. A little bit. I've never had a talent as

refined as my friends'. But I've offered my assistance whenever I could. And feeling my brother's excitement while he dreams of a future life has made me realize I should have offered it more. I remember the late-night talks Mim and I used to have, when we were in France and she insisted I needed to be more outgoing. I remember the assurances Dylan gave me in Tonga, when he told me my talent was way more useful than his own.

I remember how much Cal wished I would share my drawings with the rest of our sector, how he thought that perhaps the spirits I drew meant my ability was more than I gave it credit for.

I have always shied away from attention. Always hid in the corners of life, present when called upon but not needing to make myself unnecessarily known. Now, I wish I hadn't been so meek. I should have experienced more of the world when I could still see its shine. I should have tried to develop my talents more while I still had the ability to use my hands and sketch.

"You take the camera," I say to Kristján. My words are flat and serious as I stare at the gray of the quiet world. "You take it and you go to Amsterdam and you learn how to be *exactly* who you want."

My brother stares at me. I keep my face turned towards the ocean, but I can still sense the frown as he considers my words—and the smile as he comprehends them. He wraps an arm around my shoulder, and I take another sip of coffee.

"Do you remember," he says after a moment, "when we used to pretend we saw fairies in the fields beyond our farm?"

I grin. "You insisted that if we took their photo, we would be rich."

"We would have," he says in mock seriousness. "And famous."

We both chuckle, the sound mingling with our breaths until it all dissolves into the air around us. The tide fills the space between our words, the lapping waters our only conversation until he speaks again.

"Do you remember the first time we felt like we were truly in their presence?"

"Yes," I whisper.

My brother nods. "The air was cool and foggy, just like this. We were running and suddenly you stopped. You stared at the shadows of a tree and said someone was there. I remember the chill that slid down my spine. I remember how you looked. Scared, but in awe. I asked you what you saw, but you shook your head and wouldn't answer. That night, I found you sketching in your room. When I saw the picture, my spine tingled again. I knew it was the fairy."

"Only it wasn't a fairy," I say. "It was a ghost."

I remember that day as vividly as I remember my previous visits to this beach. Kristján and I raced and chased in turn, arguing over who was faster, both of us doubling-over with laughter when my brother tripped on a stone and fell flat on his face. I ran ahead, flying over the grass, sure if I got fast enough my feet would float. I ran further than I ever had, until I spotted the tree and stopped. The feeling came first, the feeling of creeping eyes on my back that made me spin around twice before I hid my face in my arms as if that would hide me from anyone's view. When I closed my eyes, the fairy appeared, lingering by the tree in a smoky haze. I waited for him to share his magic, until I slowly realized he had no magic to share—that he only stuck by the tree because it was where his mortal life had ended.

It was the first time I ever encountered a ghost. I was six, and Kristján was not quite eight. He has always insisted he could not sense the man like I did that day. And yet, he knew I was telling the truth. He never once faltered in his belief of what I sensed out in the field. I don't know if there is something in him—some quality of being a Sender, or perhaps a nature more intuitive than most. But it could be he is simply a good brother, one who believes in his sister when she confides a supernatural truth.

Kristján hugs tight to my shoulder before he lets his arm drop to his side as he looks again at the photos.

"The second one," he says in a quiet voice. "It's always the second one, isn't it?"

When the coffee is gone and my brother has agonized over his photos for long enough, he stands.

"You stay here," he tells me. "I want to get some scenery shots further down the beach. I'll only be a few minutes. Then we can go home."

I smile as he walks off, assuring him I will be fine on my own. My expression falls into neutral flatness when he's gone, though I have to work to keep back another smile when I hear the far-off shuttering click I know means he has snapped a final, candid shot of me before turning away. I listen to the almost imperceptible sound of his footsteps on the black sand until they are swallowed by the sloshing waves. Then I stare at the water.

My breath falls into a soft rhythm, and I try to be mindful of it—try to keep as steady a beat as I can. In, out. In, out. Self-pity wears me down, makes me feel thin-skinned and brittle. I should be grateful for what I have. I *am* grateful—for my home, my family, and my talent. But those things are slipping away from me, and sometimes it's hard to remember that there can be any joy in my existence. There's so much threatening to leave me. So many things I never got the chance to experience. Things are slipping away. And *I* am slipping away with them.

I haven't written to my friends in a while. The thought occurs to me suddenly, and with it comes the guilt of knowing how horrible the truth of it is. I stopped writing because I could no longer see the letters on my keyboard. I know how to type, and I can do it without looking. I have siblings to help me if I get stuck. Dylan and Cal both have said I could talk to them over the phone, if it makes me more comfortable. And I could do that. I could do any of those things. But I don't. Because I hate having to change my life to deal with this. Because I keep hoping that one day the problem will go away and things will be the same as they used to be. Because the self-pity is wearing me thin, and if I don't manage to break through it soon I might never get back to my old self. Because I'm—

Gray.

Because I'm slipping away.

I breathe in and out, trying to keep calm, trying to make peace with the world around me. I love this weather and this quiet ocean tide. I've always loved feeling lost in the—*gray*—fog, thinking I could float off the ground and live like a fairy in the wilds. I want to feel that way again. Grounded. *Gray.* And weightless.

He's wearing gray.

I tilt my head, turning it left and right. Kristján is wearing brown, and I am clad in blue and white. So, who am I thinking of that's wearing gray?

That's why they couldn't see him. Gray. Like the ocean.

The thought rushes in and brings with it an accompanying tidal wave of pain. I've gotten somewhat used to the headaches the doctor thinks happen when I strain my poor eyes. But this ache descends on me too fast, like a storm of needles crashing over my brain. Burning heat spreads through my forehead, and pain slams down as if someone is beating a drum against the backs of my eyes.

I groan, blinking fast and letting the world flutter around me, hoping the pain will flutter away with it like floating dirt carried off by the wind. But the hurt does not drift into the sky. It continues to hit my eyes, throbbing hard and sharp like a drumstick with a needle's edge. It taps against my eyes until the tapping hardens into a more forceful beat. Harder and harder, it beats. Then it begins to pound.

I gasp, holding my temples as the ache in my head narrows, and the pounding point turns into a strike. I cry out, clutching my head as the strike sharpens into a fierce, poker-hot stab.

I sob, wondering if my head is going to crack as the stab lengthens into a gutting slash that breaks into my eyes and slices my vision in two.

The pain rips through me, and I scream, shutting my eyes and losing my balance on the rocks. I teeter and fall, knees landing in the damp sand as my head drops so low my nose is full of the smell of earth. Gripping my glasses, I clutch at the lenses, and my own voice startles me as I scream louder than I ever thought possible. My throat burns with the force of my howling wail as the pain bloats, swells, and

then bursts through my brain in an explosion of
horrendous light.

THE PAIN GOES AWAY AS SUDDENLY AS IT APPEARED. THE SWELL DEFLATES, dissolves, and vanishes, leaving only the lingering brightness of the detonating flash. With deep, ragged breaths, I wait to make sure it is gone. When only the sound of the ocean, the feel of the cold sand, and the smell of the earth remain, I carefully open my eyes.

6

And find that the world around me is white.

7

"**KRISTJÁN!**"

I call my brother's name as I blink, over and over, trying to clear away the white as I tried to clear away the pain. My fingers come up, under the rims of my glasses, to rub at my eyes. They are clear. But I cannot see my fingers. I cannot see my body. I cannot see.

I cannot see.

"Kristján!"

I crawl forward, gripping sand in my fists and holding it up before my face. No black grains obscures the white. No shadows or impressions waver in deeper shades. There is only white, bright and unyielding. Like being totally blinded by the sun.

Raising my head, I stare at the light nothingness ahead of me. Then I scramble to my feet, moving, stumbling, and scrambling again. My body twists and my head swivels as I search for the landmarks of my surroundings. But still I see nothing but the white. Nothing but the unending blankness of a bright-blind world.

He's wearing gray.

My head turns back, hair flying in the wind as a spot of color glints to my left. With a sob of relief, I look at the man standing far away from me down the beach. He is dressed in a gray sweater, a burly thing made of wool and which, from what I can see, is heavy with damp. His pants are black. His boots too. And his head is peppered black with gray. His skin is pasty and covered with dark scruff. His eyes—brown, even from this distance I can see they are brown—are fixed in my direction.

"Hello!" I step forward more carefully, eyes trained on my goal. The man does not speak. But he keeps watching me, so I continue towards him. "Can you help me?"

All around the man is whiteness, and I myself am a disembodied mass gliding towards a single spot of life. I wish he were closer. He is far off, so distant I am surprised I can even make him out. If everything weren't white, the man would be hidden, like my brother, around a curve of tall rock. But he is there, straight before me, and the rock formations are nowhere to be found.

Gradually, I get hold of my balance and find a wobbly rhythm in my steps. I move too hard at first, stunned by the fact that I can still feel the world beneath my feet. My steps grow softer as I learn to anticipate where my foot will land. Is it still my foot? It must be. But it is no longer part of a self that I can see.

The wind breezes against my face, bringing with it a fresh smell of the ocean. I can hear the lapping of the waves to my left, although it sounds now like the water is rushing all around me. I turn my head from side to side, checking for any other sights. But the landscape does not change. There is nothing here but whiteness. Whiteness, and the man.

My foot reaches a softer squelch of mud, a pool where the tide must have reached when it was in. I step forward, into the wet, hoping the puddle is small. My boots splash gently underfoot, and I raise my hands towards the man.

"Please, can you help me?" I ask. "Can you—" My foot sinks deeper into the sand and cold seeps through my leg. I glance down at the bright nothingness, and then up again at the only source of shape and color I can see. I take another step, and the ground gives way beneath me. Cold rushes all around as I fall, slipping into the pool that is infinitely deeper than it has any right to be.

"Kornelía!" The sound of my brother comes—strangely—from behind my head. I twist my neck, looking for the person attached to the voice. My eyes squint, peering through the whiteness, while my hands splash uselessly in the frigid water and my legs kick away, trying to find a ground that's disappeared.

My brother does not appear, and my body does not find solid ground. And then it occurs to me that perhaps I am dying—that the pain in my head killed me and now I am sinking away from the living realm down into the depths of the dead. I stop moving, waiting for the final drop that will pull me wherever it is I'm supposed to go. But then loud splashing sounds close to my ear, and invisible hands grab my waist to drag me up towards the endless white sky.

"KORNELÍA!" MY BROTHER INVISIBLE, NOTHING BUT A WEIGHT PULLING against my vanished limbs—moves me out of the pool. Backward? To the side? I can't make sense of my direction anymore.

"Kristján?" I ask in a quiet voice. My hands come forward to press against his chest. The fabric of his sweater is soft, and I can smell his deodorant. His choked breath is warm against my forehead.

"What are you doing out here?" he asks. He is upset. I can sense his unease, feel his trembling. He sounds like he might be about to cry. "What are you doing?"

"That man." I turn around, and my brother holds me tight, keeping me close as I look at the man and point. "That man." I turn back against the press of my brother. "Kristján, I—I can't see."

"What?" The noise is as strangled as his breath, the exclamation one of half-disbelief and half-understanding. I can't be looking him in the eye, the way I normally would for a declaration like this. I can't see his eyes anymore to focus on them.

"There was a pain," I say, my tone surprisingly calm as I explain what occurred such a short time ago. "A headache, that worsened into a… burst. Of light. Of white. And now… I can't see anymore."

"Kornelía." He takes my hands in his, and the familiar shape of his fingers is a comfort. "Please. You can't… you have to see something. Even if you're… even then, you have see *something*. Don't you? *Don't you?*"

I squeeze his palms and shake my head. "I see white. Bright white. No shadows. No shapes. No colors. I'm… blind, Kristján. And maybe this isn't a normal kind of blind. But—" A strangled noise escapes my throat, like the wild cry of a wounded bird. "I can't see anything. Except—" I spin back to face outwards. "Except for that man."

Kristján is crying. I can sense his tears more than hear them, until I detect the sniffle when he speaks.

"What man?" he asks.

I point down the impossibly white beach. "Him. Right there. In the gray sweater."

"Kornelía…" My brother runs a hand over the back of my head to smooth my hair. It's a comforting gesture, though I'm not sure if it's meant to comfort me or him. "There's no one."

"What?" I grip his sweater tight in my fist, trying *so hard* to find his face in the white. "What?"

"You're looking at the ocean," Kristján says. He's sad. So sad it drips from him like salty splashes from the waves. "You didn't realize? You were walking into the water, Kornelía. I pulled you from the water."

Not a pool. So, I wasn't walking down the beach. I

was walking across it, to the water's edge. To the ocean.

He's wearing gray. That's why they couldn't see him. Grey, like the ocean. That's why they couldn't see him when he drowned.

"Oh."

The word leaves my lips as a breath of incomprehensible astonishment. Then, slowly, the astonishment vanishes, rolling away and washing out with the tide. "Oh," I say again, with more understanding. I close my white-seeing eyes and smile. "Oh!"

"What are—can you see again?" Kristján says in hope.

I shake my head with a laugh. "Not a thing. It's just... I've only now realized... I've seen this light before."

I thought I was in the world of the dead. Maybe I was right. Because I've seen this light before. On the nights I've helped spirits release.

"I'm blind," I say to my brother. I grip his sweater tighter and hope I am smiling in his direction. "To the *living*. But I can see the dead."

Now, it's his turn to splutter, uncomprehending of our new reality. "Th-The dead?" He sniffs again and grabs my arm. "The man you see is dead?"

I nod, glancing around at the whiteness before focusing on the only thing I see. I can't hear the man. He's too far away, perhaps, although I doubt even if I was next to him I would hear anything of what he had to say. Listening was never my talent. Seeing was. *Is.*

A memory, as vivid as the sight of the dead man, comes to me as I recall the stormy night when Reed Vodden saw an ocean-trapped ghost—and then became one himself. My elation dips as I wonder how many spirits like this are out there. Ones no one can reach. Ones no one can see.

"I can't help him," I say after a moment, wishing I could take over for my dead campmate but knowing there are others more suited to working in Reed's memory than I am. Still, that doesn't mean I can't help sometimes. This time. "But I can let someone know he's here," I continue, more to myself than to my brother. "*They* can help. And I can see. For all the ones who go unnoticed… I can *see*."

"I think we need to go home," Kristján says. "You're starting to shake. Come, Kornelía. Let's get you dry. Let's get you home."

My brother leads me further up the beach, away from the gray-clad man.

"I'll help you!" I call before I allow myself to be led away. "I will help you be free!"

I don't know if he can hear me. But the buoyancy of my own heart makes me think he must.

THE SOFT GROUND OF THE BEACH GIVES WAY TO THE HARDER DIRT OF THE road. I stumble at its change and am struck with the peculiar desire to sit down and peel off my boots. I love being barefoot, and I would have a better sense of the landscape with my skin than with the boots' numbing rubber soles. But at least I have my brother. Kristján tightens his grip until I've steadied myself. Then he walks me to the car, where our mother always leaves spare clothes in the trunk. While he waits in the driver's seat, I fumble out of my wet clothes and into baggy, soft ones that are at least three sizes too large. I don't like wearing heavy clothing, so I forgo putting on a coat in favor of wrapping a thin scarf around my neck before I crawl my fingers up the car's exterior until I'm able to push the trunk closed.

Kristján wants to help me into my seat, but I refuse his assistance. When we left home a few hours ago, my limited sight was enough to make me reach for his guiding hand. Now, I have no sight. But the car is familiar to me, its textures and odors ones I've encountered for years. I slide into the vehicle, my movements smooth and lithe. My head tilts back a little, and although the world in front of me is white—although even the insides of my own eyelids are as bright as the sun—I'm comfortable as my muscles relax against the seat. I bring my hand slowly up to the dashboard, my fingers trailing along the glove compartment, over the window buttons, and up past the lock on the door. When I touch the window's glass, its coolness sends a soft, icy spark through my fingertips, and I smile.

"We'll go home," Kristján says from beside me. His panic is so strong it is almost visible, as if the white space I know he occupies nearly ripples with his fear. I reach my hand out, far more gracefully than I did when we were in this car earlier. The whiteness awes me, as does the solidity of the world beyond the endless light. The combination makes me more careful, more aware of what space I am taking up in one plane, while I continue to watch through eyes lost in the other.

I take my brother's arm and press my fingers into the thick fabric of his sweater. He turns to me—I hear the soft crinkle of his head moving against the seat—and I do my best to exude my calm.

"It's okay," I say.

"It's not *okay*," my brother replies. He sounds incredulous, more angry than scared now. I like his anger better, but I wish he were happy instead. "You—You can't see!"

"But I *can* see," I tell him, and although I can't make

out his expression, I can sense the confusion he feels. "I can see them."

"Them." My brother scoffs. "Them… the dead?" I nod, and he scoffs again. "What good is seeing the dead if you can't see anything else, Kornelía?"

I want to explain, but I'm not quite sure how. My brothers and sisters have always accepted my talent. But that doesn't mean they truly understand it. I want to tell Kristján that, in a world of nothing but delights, I would see both living and dead with perfect clarity. But since we have to live with more balance than that, I am happy to sacrifice one thing for the other. Throughout the last two years, I have struggled against losing my eyesight—struggled to accept how the world I knew was growing hazier and hazier. But now, I exist in a different world. One of brightness. One of light. And one with a purpose. I will gladly take full clarity of the dead over uncertainty of everything. I will gladly take a world of vivid white over a world of muddled, dim shades of everything else.

I want to explain to my brother that we all have to balance our talents with what we once considered our "normal". But I don't know how. So, I only smile as I hold his arm.

"It's okay," I say again. "Let's go home, Kristján. You don't have to worry about me anymore. I'm good now. Let's go home."

My hand drops to my lap. After a long pause, Kristján starts the ignition.

10

Ten minutes into our drive home, I raise my hand to brush tickling hair from my face. When I do, my fingers hit against the frames of my thick glasses, and I start to laugh.

"What is it now?" Kristján asks, his words wary.

I pull off the frames and turn in my brother's direction. "I just realized something terrific," I say, my face stretched wide with my grin. "I am *finally* able to throw these horrid glasses away!"

For a moment, my brother is silent. Then he too starts to laugh. I hear the window lower, feel the rush of cold from outside the car.

"Go ahead," Kristján says in the conspiratorial voice meant only for sneaking around the mystical wild.

I stare at the whiteness where my glasses should be and hope the fairies won't begrudge me this act of littering. My arm moves until it's out in the rushing, windswept cold.

I let the glasses go.

MEANDER

tortured with?"

Wrapped in a blanket to ward off the damp chill from the rain outside my leaky window, my voice sounds as sleepy as the rest of me as I mumble my words and struggle to keep my eyes open. It's nearly two in the bloody morning, and I need to go to bed. But I hold on, like I always do. Because this is the best part of my day—the best part of every day—and I don't want to say goodbye.

On the computer, Cal smiles, his head propped in one hand as he lays on his comforter. "We don't have any traditions," he says.

"Everyone has traditions," I argue.

He raises a half-white eyebrow. "You don't."

"I don't count," I say. "We don't actually do the whole *Christmas* thing around here."

Cal gives me a dubious look, then shrugs. "We

watch movies and bake cookies," he says. He raises his head, looking off to the side of the screen as he contemplates the subject at hand. "We always go to my grandma's house for a family thing too. But there's nothing set in stone. When my grandpa was still alive, there was more of a tradition, I guess. We'd go to his and Grandma's house on Christmas Eve, and he'd play the violin. I only remember about two years of him doing that, but my mom told me he always did it while she was growing up."

He looks back at the screen, his expression soft and wistful as he recollects his Christmases past. I want to reach through the computer and touch his cheek, his neck. I imagine the warmth of his skin while the cold seeps through my window and, outside, some lunatic on a motorbike revs their engine for the whole street to hear.

"He died at the beginning of December," Cal continues. "But it was on Christmas Eve that I really, you know… *felt* it. Grandma came to our house, and on the twenty-fourth, she gave me his violin as an early present. She asked me to play something. And that's when it hit me. He was gone, and his violin was now mine. I wish I'd gotten the chance to have another Christmas with him. It's been so long I can barely remember what it sounded like when he played."

"I'm sorry you didn't get more time with him," I say.

Cal folds his arms to settle against them, and soon the wistful expression fades into a pointed stare. "Okay, so you don't have any traditions. But is there anything you'd *like* to do while you're here? Something Christmassy you've always secretly longed to take part in?"

"I don't like Christmas." I hitch the blanket tighter around my shoulders and poke one finger towards the screen. "And if you try to convert me by making us go bloody carolling, I'm never visiting you again."

His whole face lights up as he laughs. "Why would you think I'd ever go *carolling*?"

I scoff through my smile, half-breath and half-sound as I lean closer to the screen. "Because you've probably got some baroque Christmas carol memorized for your violin, and you'll want me for the choir part to make the experience authentic."

"Well, there *are* some spectacular pieces from that era," he says, his amusement already curbing into serious contemplation. "Handel, Vivaldi, Bach… all the greats crafted compositions for the season. Corelli's concerto is quite festive, but I don't know if there's a vocal compon—"

"Cal!" I cut him off with a laugh, and he blinks out of his thoughts, his smile dropping into a look of embarrassment when he realizes he's wandered off on a musical tangent.

"Right," he says as the embarrassment gives way and he remembers what we were discussing. "No carolling, I promise. But there has to be something. Some movie you actually love even though you insist you've never watched it. Or some gift you've secretly always cherished." He grins. "I know you too well. You aren't a total humbug. There's got to be an inkling of Christmas cheer somewhere under all that grumpiness."

I slink down in my seat, my eyes fixing on the deep scratches in my rickety desk. My teeth run over my bottom lip as I glance back up at the computer.

"There's one thing," I admit.

Across the ocean, Cal sits up on his elbows and scoots closer to his screen.

"Tell me," he says, his smile far too perky for the middle of the night—*my* middle of the night, anyway. "And *don't* mumble," he adds in a sterner voice.

I sigh and sit up straighter, shaking the curls from my eyes as I think of the pathetic holidays of my childhood.

"We never had any such thing as a family Christmas," I say. "Growing up, Liam and I usually got a few pieces of clothing. My aunt would sometimes send money, but Mum kept that for herself. If we were lucky, our out of touch but well-meaning gran would send us a toy meant for toddlers or something that needed a million batteries we couldn't afford."

"If you were *lucky*?" he asks.

I smirk. "Liam would hock those for a few pounds so we could get a takeaway from the high street." I shrug one shoulder, clutching at the blanket as it starts to slip. "Mum never gave a damn about the holidays. But the *one* thing she always did was to give Liam a chocolate orange. Thought she was Father Christmas for that, she did. She'd be so smug, making a big deal about it being *his* present—his reward for not being the unwanted child. I wasn't allowed to have any of it. But once she was distracted by the telly or had got into her booze, Liam would call me to his room. He'd smash the orange and divide the pieces, and he'd let me have half. He never short-changed me, even though it was his gift. He always split it even."

I tilt my head back, eyes closing as I talk. "When I was little, I held out hope that one year maybe Mum would give me a chocolate too. When I got older and Liam moved out—and any pretence of Christmas festivities died—I decided that someday, when I had money of my own, I'd buy a damned orange and eat the whole thing myself. But then I grew up and realized that saving my money for things like cross-continent plane tickets is more important than a bit of chocolate. Priorities, yeah?"

The soft recollection has made my mind foggy. When I finish my grand explanation, I drift into a silence that almost drifts into sleep until Cal speaks.

"Meander?"

"Mmm?" I mumble.

When he doesn't respond, I force my eyes open and find him watching me. His eyes are bright and his smile is soft, and the sight of his happiness makes every one of my nerves tingle.

"You're coming here tomorrow," he half-whispers when our gazes catch.

"Says you." I turn my monitor so it picks up the cracked screen of the alarm clock on my nightstand. "It's after two here. According to my clock, I'm coming there today."

I twist the monitor back, and for a moment neither of us speaks. He stares at me and I stare at him, and no words are needed to make my room warmer, the lunatic on the motorbike quiet, or the whole stupid world a nicer place to be.

"Get some sleep," he says after a while.

I nod, the blanket slipping as I stretch my arms over my head. "Enjoy your evening of baroque Christmas music."

Cal's face flushes as he laughs, and I'm pleased to

know I've caught him out on what he plans to do with his night. I grab the blanket and toss it on my bed. Then I focus on the monitor so I can perform the unpleasant task of ending our call.

"I miss you," Cal says, his laughter shifting into a voice that is intimate and low. "But I'll see you soon."

"Soon," I repeat, my eyes fixed on his.

Soon, I'll be away from this cold, damp house, with its leaky windows and broken furniture. Soon, I'll be away from the noisy neighbors and the mother who is disgusted by the very sight of me. Soon, I'll be away from this hellhole of a street and this country full of vile ghosts.

Soon, I'll be in Canada, where I'll finally be back with Cal.

My sleep is brought to an abrupt end by the sound of the blaring television, and on the morning of my flight I'm graced with a delightfully grating headache as soon as I roll out of bed. I shower, scrounge the kitchen for food we don't have, then spend half an hour fighting with Mum, who has suddenly decided she's not going to let me leave home for the Christmas break. After reminding her I paid for my own ticket—a statement that is only half true since Cal and I shared the cost between us—she snatches away the packet of crisps I managed to find in the cupboard and wails on about me being an ungrateful waste of space. I sit on the sofa, trying my best to block out her voice, until the neighbor starts to pound on the wall. When Mum rounds on him instead, I use the moment of distraction to retreat to my room and climb out the window so I can run halfway across town to reach the station before my bus to London takes off without me.

I spend hours on the bus, push through crowds in the Underground, and wind through an airport full of impatient travellers. After getting my ticket, I change my route to the terminal twice in order to avoid ghosts, then wait by my gate in tense worry that my flighty behavior will have set the security team on my watch. When the plane boards, I annoy the other passengers by walking the entire length of the cabin to make sure the place isn't haunted before I settle into my seat. Only when the flight finally takes off do I try to relax— and end up spending most of the ensuing eight hours fending off the woman in the seat next to me who is entirely too curious about my choices in books.

It takes too many hours, too many inconveniences, and way too many people to reach the damned arrivals gate in Toronto. But I know I'd go through the whole sodding mess again when the glass doors slide open and I see his face.

Callum Silver stands close to the railed exit ramp, grinning like an idiot as soon as he spots me. A beautiful idiot, who genuinely thought he should tell me what he was going to wear so I'd be able to find him in the crowd. Like his deep blue eyes and white streaks of hair weren't enough to make him stand out. Like I wouldn't be able to find him in any crowd, anywhere in the world.

My whole body feels lighter when I walk down the ramp. I want to wrap Cal in my arms and snog his gorgeous face off, but his parents stand a few steps back staring at me with wary curiosity, so I hug him instead while he breathes his hello against my neck. The motion is too short and too casual. But when I feel his weight against me, I know that our decision—

the weeks of planning, the pooling of our money, the making of arrangements so I could spend Christmas in Canada at his home—was worth every aggravation the world can throw my way.

I suffer through the hour-long car ride to Cal's house, his parents making idle small chat until we stop for coffee and tea and use the beverages as an excuse to let the car settle into silence. When we finally make it to his street, I feel the first nudges of stupid Christmas cheer at the sight of so many brick houses strung with lights, the yards white with more snow than I've ever seen. But the real test to my sour disposition comes when we are inside and granted a few moments of privacy in Cal's room. Touching him and smelling him after so long a deprivation makes me smile so much my cheeks actually start to hurt. One taste of his lips, and I'm tempted to announce a lifelong admiration for the holiday season that brought us back together.

The first week of my trip speeds by in an overwhelming whirl of anxious emotions. I sit down to dinner with his family that first night, too nervous to eat much but trying hard to make sure I don't eat so little they stare at my plate with suspicious concern. Cal's sister Rose interrogates me about ghosts, despite her brother's warnings to shut up and their parents' obvious unease about the topic at hand. By the time the dishes are cleared and dessert is served, my gut's so riled I don't think I can deal with any more food. But the apple crumble placed before me turns out to be delicious, and after looking awkwardly between his parents to compliment whichever one of them made it, I'm rewarded with the unexpected delight of seeing Cal blush as his mother explains that *he* was the one to make it—just to celebrate my arrival.

And bloody hell, if that doesn't make the whole painful meal worth it. Especially once we're alone after everyone else goes to bed, and I am able to fully express my appreciation for this newly discovered talent.

Time zone changes and feeling out of place in such a big house keep me restless the whole of the first night. But when I startle awake, panicked at the thought of how much I don't want to mess this trip up, I turn my head and see Cal sleeping next to me, both of us curled together in his bed since the door is locked and no one will know I'm not actually sleeping in the cot on the floor. The warmth of someone's body next to my own is a peculiar sensation I've only experienced one other time, back in Guatemala when the two of us had a few hours of sleep before we were hauled back to Greenland so we could get booted home early from camp. I remember that other time, replaying the things the two of us accomplished together. Then I move my head closer to his and drift back to sleep.

For five days I stay in a perpetual swing of turmoil and bliss. Hours around his too-cautious parents are countered by the hours when they go to work, Rose goes to school, and Cal skips his classes so we can explore his city or stay tucked away together in the warmth of his room. There are evenings of Rose-led dinner conversations and holiday movie watching next to the big tree crowded with gifts, followed by quiet midnight conversations under the bedcovers, Cal and mine's nightly routine continued with the brilliant addition of not having a computer screen to keep us apart.

There are moments I catch his mother staring at

the scar on my jaw or see the shift in his father's look whenever Rose—who switches conversation topics like I flip the pages of a book—goes from talking about her day at school to telling Cal about one of her friends' supposed run-ins with a ghost. And then there are moments when I stare into Cal's eyes and almost tell him the thing I keep promising myself I will say before this trip's end, the thing I say in my head over and over every time he smiles and tells me how glad he is that I'm here.

When his lips press to mine, I know it's worth *every* moment of unease or annoyance to have *any* moment like this with him. It's worth all the apprehension my body could possibly contain.

Cal makes every moment worth it. Every bloody one.

Until the night before Christmas arrives.

On December twenty-fourth, we stand outside of his family car on route to attend a Christmas party Cal couldn't wiggle us out of. A family party, full of relatives and memories of all the holidays that have come before. A special party, because it's the last one that will take place in this old house with its warm white lights strung over the roofline and around the evergreen in the front yard that's rooted next to the realtor's SOLD sign.

This is Cal's grandmother's house. This is the home where Cal used to spend the Christmas Eves of his childhood, listening to his grandfather play the violin. And now, we're supposed to go inside.

And I have to tell him why I can't.

Because my air is already starting to close off as something squeezes my neck. Because my arm stings. Because my jaw itches and burns.

And this, right here, might be the moment that makes this trip not worth it. Because this house is haunted. Because Cal doesn't know there's a ghost inside.

Because I have a horrible feeling it's not just his grandmother I'm about to meet.

3

"CAL."

After his parents and sister have started towards the door, I tug on his sleeve and try not to sound like I need to clear my throat. He turns back to me, his face void of the strained wariness I'm used to from others. His curious eyes only fill with concern when he sees the panic in my stare.

"What's wrong?" he asks, his voice low so the rest of his family won't hear. They reach the front step without looking back at us. I stay firmly by the car, and Cal stands a step away from me, poised to turn but staying still until he hears my complaint.

"I… I can't go in there," I say.

Cal glances at the house with its bright lights and murmuring noises echoing from within. The street is lined with cars, and apparently this get together usually has about thirty people in attendance. I haven't been thrilled about the idea of going to a party, but until this moment the event was only another push of the swing, a necessary evil to allow for the unadulterated pleasure of the moments leading up to—and away from—this night.

When he looks back at me, I can tell Cal is wondering if I'm just trying to hide. Which, to be fair, I do a lot. I don't like people. I don't like crowds. And there is unquestionably a tug of desire now that's independent of the ghost, a soft yearning to duck away from the car and head down the street to find somewhere halfway warm to sit and read until the night is over.

But I wouldn't do that, not with him here, and not with his parents already uncertain about my presence as their son's quiet friend who also claims to see the dead. I don't like people. But I like Cal. I much more than *like* Cal, and I want to make as decent an impression on his family as I can. Which means I can't go into this bloody house. I can't ruin the entire party by being choked unconscious while a ghost throws a tantrum and smashes the fine china.

"It won't be that bad…" Cal starts, before he sighs. "Okay, it will be awful. But it's always awful, and it's only for a few hours, and…"

When I shake my head, his words taper off and he gives me a harder look—first at my mouth and then at my chest, as if he can see the shallow rise and fall through the winter coat he's letting me wear because I came inadequately prepared for this northern cold.

"Boys?" his mother calls from the doorstep, and Cal looks at his family while I do my best to appear calm and not utterly pissed off that I can't manage a single outing without messing everything up.

"We'll be in soon," Cal says. He sounds less certain

than he should, and his parents eye with him with a cautious distrust that pisses me off even more. They don't ask if he's okay, if I'm okay, if either one of us would like the car keys so we don't have to wait in the cold. They just glance between us and then lower their eyes like the very thought of what sort of crisis we're having embarrasses them.

"Well, hurry up," she says. She grabs Rose by the shoulder, Cal's sister the only one of the three that looks like she wants to know more about what is going on. But her parents don't give her time to ask questions. They usher her inside, then close the door without looking back.

When the door is shut, I slump against the side of the car and put my hands over my face.

"You feel something?" Cal asks. When I lower my hands, I discover he's moved nearer to me, and I push off the car to lean into him, close enough the clouds of our breath mingle.

"Yes," I say. I hold onto the lapel of the oversized coat he's borrowing from his dad, afraid—always a little afraid—he's going to slip away from me. "I'm so sorry. I didn't... I wanted tonight to be..."

"Meander," Cal says, and to my relief he smiles. "You can't help it. We don't get that choice. But—" he pauses, glancing over his shoulder at the house. "Are you sure it's here? Not another house on the street? Not the one next door or something?"

I shake my head again, gripping tighter to his coat with one hand while the fingers of the other come up to stroke along his ear.

"Cal, I'm sorry," I say again. "It's this house. It's..."

He frowns, knowing I have more information

than he does and trying to guess at what I might be about to say. I want him to figure it out for himself and, on most days, I'd be more than content to wait until he does. Cal doesn't catch onto things the way I do, and I know it bugs him. But watching him try to work something out is peculiarly lovely. He doesn't look vacant or annoyed like most people do when they don't understand what I'm trying to convey. His expression shifts into one of steady concentration, his blue eyes turning nearly gray as he focuses on breaking apart my words like he's crafting with the utmost care, fitting the phrases one way and then the other to see what outcome makes the most sense.

Under normal circumstances, I'd watch the serenity of Cal's mind at work until I caught the fleck of frustration in his gaze. But this is too important to drag out.

"Have there been other people who have lived here?" I ask in as unaffected a voice as I can manage. "Anyone before your grandparents moved in?"

I'd be thrilled if my intuition proved incorrect and I discovered this house has been lived in by dozens of families in the decades since it was built. But I don't get the satisfaction of being wrong. As soon as I ask the question, Cal shakes his head.

"No," he says. "They moved here when the house was new. They were the first—" He stops, eyes casting to the house before his whole body shifts to face me. He searches my gaze and I watch as, inch by inch, the truth covers him like the thick blanket of snow at our feet.

I want to wrap my arms around his waist and pull him in against me, but I'm terrified that if I move he'll struggle away. So I stand still as his lips press tight and his eyes start to swim, the black and white lashes tangling with tears that he quickly wipes away with the back of his hand.

"It can't be," he whispers.

My own eyes start to sting, so I focus on breathing and make myself bring a hand up to his cheek. He turns his face into my palm before stepping in and dropping his head onto my shoulder. I lower my arm and hug him as tightly as I can through our coats, mumbling apologies I know don't mean a thing.

When he lifts his head, his eyes find mine again. "My grandfather?"

I nod, wishing so much that I didn't have to, that this was only a stolen moment out in the snow where I could kiss him and wonder if perhaps the Christmas season is worth celebrating after all. But all the pinches of festive joy I've felt over the past week have just been proven to be rubbish. This isn't a romantic scene where I confess the full truth of my feelings for this boy and then snog him so fiercely we both wind up laughing as we fall into the snow. The holidays suck, and so does our reality.

No matter how hard we try, we can't escape being Senders. And being a Sender—like the Christmas season itself—is absolute shit.

"OKAY," CAL SAYS AFTER A MOMENT. HE SNIFFS AND WIPES MORE TEARS from his eyes. "What… what do we do? Do you want to leave?"

I do want to leave. Of course I do. And if I tell him right now that we should go, he'll find a way to make it happen. But my ears are ringing with the question he hasn't asked, and it's the harder question to answer. If we leave, what happens to his grandfather? If his grandfather is a ghost—has been a ghost since Cal was a little kid—how much longer will it be before someone else with an ability like mine comes around?

I don't want to put myself through this. Not ever. But certainly not here in a house full of partygoers that also happen to be relatives of the most important person in my life. And the thing is, Cal doesn't want me to go through it, either. I know he doesn't, because I know he actually gives a damn about whether I'm okay. He actually understands what it's like to *not* be okay because of how messed up seeing spirits is.

But it's his bloody grandpa, and I can't leave him with the knowledge that the man who meant so much to him—the one who gave him his violin—has been lingering in misery for over a decade waiting for someone to notice his presence. My eyes slide to the realtor's sign on the front yard. This is the last time Cal's grandmother will have a Christmas party in her house. She's downsizing, which means come the new year, this house will belong to strangers and Cal won't even be able to come here in hopes he might have some effect.

Shit. It's absolute shit. Because there's no way I'm going to drop that sort of suffering on him.

"No," I say in response to his question. It's a lie. But it's also the truth. "I want to see him."

Cal's probably got as many conflicting emotions as I do. His eyes light up when I announce my decision to help instead of running away, but he doesn't look happy with my choice. If anything, he looks guilty, as if he's the one making me do this. Proof of how utterly idiotic relationships can be. Here we are, face to face on opposite ends of a problem, solely because neither one of us wants the other one to feel any pain.

"Not like we have anywhere else to go, anyway," I say with a shrug that's convincingly casual, even if he knows I'm full of it. "And it's cold out here."

"It'll be cold in there too," Cal replies.

"True," I say. I give the house a scrutinizing stare. "Your grandmother have a fireplace?"

Cal winces, knowing I'm not in search of warmth. "Yeah. Gas, not wood. That better or worse?"

"Can't say," I sigh. "Just the one?"

"Yes," he replies. "In the living room. That's where the party will be."

"Good," I say. Then I sigh again. "So long as we're far enough away from the living room that none of the party-goers catches on fire."

The words are totally serious, and Cal knows it. But he cracks a smile, and soon we're both laughing—until my breath catches and turns into a wheezing cough. Cal waits to make sure I'm getting enough air in my lungs. Then his eyes roam my face, looking for a certainty I do my best to project.

"Thank you," he murmurs after a moment. I nod, and he pushes me lightly against the car so I can share my breath with his.

When Cal steps back, I swallow hard, determined not to show how winded I've become. "Anytime," I whisper. My breath is more ragged than I'd like. But he still graces me with a final, soft kiss before stepping back.

"So," he says, grabbing my hand as he looks at his grandmother's home, "how are we going to do this?"

I survey the house, its mid-century exterior practically shining with holiday cheer. The structure is two storeys, which means we can hopefully do this a floor apart from the other guests. Of course, that all depends on where the ghost likes to reside. This was his house, apparently from the time it was built. That might mean he has free reign of the place. But some spirits are stubborn, and I can't count on his trailing wherever I lead. Unfortunately, I won't know one way or the other until we're inside.

"We need to be away from everyone else, if at all possible," I say. My throat hurts, aching like I've gone for a really horrid run. I try not to swallow too many times, try to breathe as normally as possible without gulping for air. "And anything we can do to avoid notice would be great. A good escape route would also be welcome. You know, in case…"

Cal nods. He stares at the front door and then nods again.

"I'll get Rose," he says at last. "She can be our distraction. She's the youngest kid in the family, so people are always happy to pay attention to her. She'll help us—wait here."

He bounds for the house, and I retreat down the sidewalk until I can breathe without restraint. After a minute or two has passed, the door opens and Cal beckons me forward. I steel myself against the inevitable, hoping Rose will be successful in diverting attention from me. I don't need to be watched, and it'll be hell if someone with good intentions but zero understanding calls for a paramedic when things get really bad.

Because they will get bad. There's no doubt about that.

I breathe the last full breath I can. Then I walk up to the house, my eyes fixed on Cal, grateful that this time I have him by my side.

 quickly masked by a coolness different from what I experienced outside. The house still smells nice, at least, like apple cider spiced with cloves. I'd love a cup of something warm before the cold really sets in. But we don't have time for any frivolities like mingling with the crowd or sampling the finger foods that are probably spread around the living room on platters made of gold.

We wipe snow off our shoes but keep them on in case we need to make a speedy exit from the house. We keep our coats on as well, though Cal does unwrap his red-plaid scarf from around my neck to temporarily sling around his own. My coat is not high-collared, and I wore the scarf in place of a turtleneck to keep my scar hidden away. I don't like it on display. But Cal knows what it looks like far better than I do, and it's probably a good call not to have something around my neck that could easily be pulled tight.

Rose is in the foyer, her fingers trailing the leaves of a poinsettia as she waits for our arrival. When she hears us enter, her eyes alight on her big brother, her smile excited for whatever task she's been enlisted for. Rose is a good kid. She's too curious for her own good, perhaps, and she definitely talks too much. But she doesn't look at Cal the way their parents do, the way so many people do when they notice the marks of our unique brushes with death. Even when her eyes catch on my neck, she only looks at the rope scars with more curiosity. Maybe it's because she's too young to make the assumptions most people made when that particular ghost attacked. Or maybe she actually believes us when we say we talk to ghosts—no matter what her parents say to one another when they think their children can't hear.

"Is there really a ghost here?" she asks me, before Cal hushes her and she remembers to lower her voice. "Our grandpa?" She doesn't sound bothered by the prospect, but then again, I doubt she would be. Cal's grandfather died before she was born. She never even knew the man now hovering around this house.

"Yes, there's a ghost," Cal says in my place. I can't talk much right now. I've got to focus on breathing, on keeping calm and not worrying about the pain slicing through my old wounds. At least the last four months have been uneventful. I've worked myself into a routine at home, one that keeps me fairly well out of spirits' ways. Cal's the same, both of us always careful about where we go and what we do. I sometimes wonder if it will ever be any different. But this past week *has* been different. I've gone to loads of places I don't normally go, comfortable to explore with Cal at my side. It's amazing what having a partner can do. It's amazing what a difference going from one to two makes.

"There's no one upstairs," Rose says. "I already checked. If Mom or Dad asks, I'll tell them…" She struggles, not remembering what she's supposed to say. Cal sighs and grabs her shoulders, angling her towards the living room.

"Stay away from Mom and Dad," he says. "As much as possible. Then they're not likely to ask at all. If they do, say we were here, but that we went for a walk to get away from the crowds."

"Right." Rose stops at the edge of the hallway and looks back at us. "Are you sure I can't come and watch?"

"*No*," Cal says. He waves his arms, and she rolls her eyes before disappearing into the living room. When she's gone, he turns to me. "How are you doing?"

"Okay," I say. "Better if we get this over with."

"Right," Cal says, echoing his sister's word. He turns towards the staircase and starts up. "Let me know where you want to go. Or, if you want to leave. Or, if you *need* to leave."

I smile, my hand hovering at his back to keep what little touch I can. "I will."

We walk up the stairs, the music, clinking glasses, and happy chatter of the crowded living room fading into dim ambiance as we reach the second floor. As much as I dislike crowds, the noises from below would make a cheery companion to this scene, if it weren't for the flare of pain and squeeze on my neck when we reach the second-storey landing. I take a moment to grip onto the banister, struggling to catch a rhythm of breath before I point down the hall.

"He's over there," I say.

Cal's mouth is closed tight as we cross the length of the hallway and stop outside of a closed door. "This is their bedroom," he says at last. "Or, uh, it was. I guess it's Grandma's now. Or… Or I guess it actually still belongs to them both." He lets the truth of the words settle over him. Then he shakes his head and grabs the doorknob.

The room is dark. I want to turn on the light, but there's no point. If we keep the switch off, perhaps the ghost won't be so quick to use up the room's energy and drain what other power this house has got. There are a lot of people downstairs. I don't want to end the party by throwing the house into darkness so soon. So, I keep the light off as I step inside, longing for a second of stillness I don't get. The ghost is already present, hovering across from me in full, wispy glory. My breath hitches and I shiver as Cal closes the door behind us.

I learned an important lesson last summer. My talent has shifted, and now it's not only angry ghosts I see. But if I'm already viewing Cal's grandfather with this much clarity, it means the emotions coursing through the smoky mass are fierce.

It means that—whatever this spirit is feeling— things are about to go from bad to worse.

CAL DOESN'T NEED TO ASK IF I CAN SEE THE GHOST. AS SOON AS WE'RE IN THE room, I stagger back against the closed door and he comes to my side, both of us shaking with cold.

"Where is he?" Cal asks, and I point towards the far side of the room where the ghost is standing in wait. The energy I felt when entering the house is more intense now, but it's not as concentrated as I would have expected. Instead, it's dispersed all around us, giving the whole room a feeling of instability, like everything is vibrating so slightly it's undetectable to the human eye. Nothing has moved from its place yet, which is good. But the tremor is present, even if it's slight. I can't afford to take the relative quiet for granted.

"He's tall," I manage between small gulps of air. "Broad shoulders. A… A beard? Some sort of facial hair."

Cal nods. "That's him," he says in a weird voice that's half as strangled as my own. He stares in the general direction of the ghost, before he turns away and stares instead at the door. "Damn. I never thought…"

"You never felt anything?" I ask.

"No." Cal presses a fist to his mouth before dropping his arm and swinging back around to face the rest of the room. "I didn't come here last Christmas. Before that…" he lets out a choked laugh. "It was always a bit cold here. I just thought Grandma didn't do much with the heating."

I wish I could comfort him. I want to wrap him in my arms and hold him so tight the warmth of my blood erases the cold of this dead room. I want to— but I can't. Right now, I have to focus on keeping my breath. And listening to the ghost. Because he's starting to talk. And although the name is so familiar to me, it takes a moment before the word gets through the low rifling that's started deep in my brain.

"*Callum?*" the ghost asks, and I realize why it is his energy has been subdued. He doesn't have well-defined eyes. But his head is looking our way, and it's not me the gaze is turned towards.

"He's asking about you," I say. Cal looks at me, surprise in his eyes as I nod at the ghost. "Yes," I say to the old man. "It's him."

The ghost comes forward, and I flinch back in pain and expectation. But he stops a foot away from Cal, watching his grandson. Cal hugs his coat to him, sniffing in the cold.

"What does he need?" he asks.

I tilt my head back against the door, closing my eyes and trying to see if I can work it out without asking the question. I don't want the ghost's attention on me. But there's nothing defined in my head, and it soon becomes apparent I won't be able to pick up on his needs without a little nudge.

"We're here to help you," I say to the ghost after giving up my own internal search. "Cal and me both. Tell us why you're still here."

I'd hoped Cal's being so near might continue to keep the spirit calm. But once the question is asked, the ghost's energy shifts and crackles, and the pain on my arm flares while my throat constricts, and I begin to cough. Cal steps closer to my side, but there's nothing he can do except pull me out of the room. That's not an option. Not yet. For now, we both have to stay put.

Spirits don't talk to me as readily as they seem to do for Cal. They'll speak, sometimes. But often they stay fairly quiet. Cal's grandfather stays quiet now, but the tremor of energy in the room grows to a visible shaking of the knickknacks on the dresser and the lampshade next to the bed. I can't tell what emotion this ghost is holding onto, but I'm fairly sure it's not anger. If it were, the large picture frame above the bed would not still be hanging on the wall.

"Did he say anything?" Cal asks. I shake my head, and he stares at the spot where the ghost is. "Grandpa?" He pauses and glances back at me. "I feel like an idiot, by the way. Is he over there still?"

I manage a little smile and a nod. "By the nightstand," I croak.

Cal looks troubled by the sound of my voice. He gives me a worried once-over, before he again faces the ghost.

"Grandpa," he says. "It's Cal, uh, Callum. Your grandson. I didn't know you were here. I'm sorry for that. If I'd known... Anyway, you can't stay here, Grandpa. You're not meant to. And besides, Grandma's leaving, did you know? The house is up for sale. She's downsizing to something smaller. Closer to us, so Mom can keep an eye."

At the mention of the sale, the ghost's energy picks up again, this time a full shift to kick things into high gear. I gasp, choke, and sink down to the ground against the door while the picture on the wall starts to rattle and even the wood bed frame begins to shake. Cal grabs onto the footboard, pressing down as if he can stop the movement, while the knickknacks on the dresser roll and clatter to the floor.

The feeling comes over me in a wash, the notes of the emotion finally settling into place. The ghost is not angry, but frustrated. Frustrated about the move, maybe, which could explain why Cal never really noticed his presence before. But the ghost didn't just pop back from the other side because he's pissed that someone's selling his home. He's been here all along, which means the move is not the motivation for his frustration—it's only a catalyst to make it worse.

"There's something that needs doing before she can leave," I wheeze, and it takes so much out of me I have to close my eyes and let my head drop to my chest.

The ghost likes my response. While Cal comes back to my side, asking me questions of whether he needs to get me out, my head fills with the turbulent rushing of flapping paper, like thousands of pages flipping by at high speed while I try to recall something I've read—*anything* I've read—that might somehow relate to what this spirit needs.

I cover my eyes, pressing against the strained ache of searching and the lightheaded intensity of not getting enough air. The pages rush by, one after another, until they stop so abruptly it's like whiplash in my brain. I drop my hands to my sides as the story comes to me in a flash, the intensity of it so bright my eyes fly open and my breath leaves for a disturbingly long pause while the bed begins to thump against the floorboards and, behind my head, someone pounds on the door.

7

I'M TRYING SO HARD TO BREATHE THAT I DON'T EVEN REALIZE I'VE barricaded the door with my weight. With a muttering of curses, Cal grabs onto my waist and hauls me forward, both of us tumbling to the floor before he rolls and scrambles up. He pulls open the door and asks whoever is outside for help. Black clouds form on either side of my head, and I barely comprehend the feeling of being dragged out into the hallway.

The world around me goes hazy, and I stare at the gray sort of nothing while I try to pull air into my lungs.

"Shit," Cal says. He bends over me, but I can only make out the outline of his face. "*Shit.* I need to brush up on my CPR. Meander, can you hear me?"

"Is he dead?" a high voice I'm pretty sure belongs to Rose asks.

"Shut up," Cal says. He grabs his phone and throws it to his sister. "Look up how to do CPR. Quick."

He bends back over me and tilts up my chin, the

small movement enough to finally let the air back in. I suck in breath and then cough it out, rolling onto my side and gasping while Cal rubs my back.

"That was scary," Rose says from beside us.

"No kidding," he says. He brushes curls away from my face so he can look at me. "Are you all right? Do you need help? Should I still do CPR?"

I roll onto my back again and smile at him. "I'm okay." My throat burns, and my head hurts. I take several ragged, harsh breaths and put an arm over my eyes to help me focus.

"When we get home, I'll enrolling in a first aid course," he says as he lets out a huff of breath.

I laugh. "I hear "Stayin' Alive" is a great accompaniment for chest compressions."

Cal hits me on the shoulder. "It's not funny, you ass. You scared me."

"I know, I'm sorry." I lift my arm and struggle to sit up. He helps to prop me against the wall, and I glance over to where Rose is standing in her sparkling red Christmas dress, still clutching her brother's phone.

"Did the ghost do that?" she asks, and the question is so innocently genuine both of us start to laugh.

"Yeah, he did," I say in my raw voice.

Rose tilts her head to one side. "I thought so. Mom and Dad gave me the evil eye when all that noise started. You're gonna be in big trouble, Cal. Everyone heard it."

"You weren't supposed to talk to them!" Cal snaps.

"I didn't!" His sister throws up her hands in surrender. "I was across the room. Everyone started asking what the noise was, and Mom and Dad found me by the kitchen door. Honest, I didn't say a thing.

They just assumed it was you."

He groans. "What did you hear?"

"A bunch of rattling," Rose says. "Like a really powerful vacuum or something."

Cal sweeps a hand up over his head, not quite touching his hair but making sure it's still in place— an automatic gesture he does whenever he's trying to think.

"I found out what the ghost needs," I say, and his eyes snap to mine.

"You did?"

"Some of it." I shrug. "There's something hidden. Something your grandmother needs to find. I think he's been waiting a long time for her to find it, and now he's getting frustrated that she'll leave before she does."

"Hidden?" Cal repeats the word, his expression thoughtful as he tries to make the concept connect with anything in his memory.

"Like a treasure?" Rose asks. She bounces on her toes, evidently excited by the prospect of such an adventurous turn to the night's events.

"No," Cal says.

"Sort of," I say at the same time. He looks at me, and I shrug again. *The Secret of Chimneys*. Agatha Christie. In the story, there's a jewel hidden at a house. A house with a… a gathering going on. There's got to be some resemblance to your grandfather's unfinished business, if that's what I'm picking up on."

"Can I help you search for it?" Rose asks.

Cal sits beside me, his head against the wall and bewilderment shining in his eyes. "A treasure," he mumbles to himself. "He's a ghost, and he's got a hidden treasure. And now we have to do an undead scavenger hunt on Christmas Eve." He passes a hand over his face and glances at me. "Why is our life so ridiculous?"

I smile, sorry he's going through this but happy he considers it a burden for us both, that he counts our separate lives as one to be shared. I wish there was no spirit in this house. But if there has to be, I'm glad we're both here, where I can take the brunt of the pain and he can drag me out whenever I'm in need of air. Our life *is* ridiculous. It's bloody ludicrous. But if we've got to spend our Christmas Eve releasing family ghosts, then I'm sure as hell happy we get to do it together.

"It wouldn't be much of a shindig without a few party games," I say.

Cal laughs, a sound which turns into a groan halfway through. He shakes his head and looks at Rose.

"You can't go back down yet," he says to his sister. "And the sooner we find whatever's hidden, the better."

"So that means I can help?" she asks.

"Yes," Cal says with a sigh. "So long as you listen."

"I'm not five, Cal," Rose says with the assured annoyance of someone who sounds more like a teenager than a nine-year-old.

Call rolls his eyes and then gets to his feet. He stands over me, looking bothered by the words he's about to say.

"You didn't happen to catch where this treasure is hidden, did you?" he asks without any real hope.

I shake my head and reach out my arms so he can help me up.

"Not a clue," I mumble. My breathing is much better out here, almost as clear as it was in the front yard. This ghost is not full of malice, which is a relief.

I can take a bit of frustration. Frustration is less likely to result in a new burning scar.

"How are we supposed to look for treasure, if we don't know where it is?" Rose asks.

Cal retrieves his phone from her grasp, while I turn again to the bedroom door.

"We have to go back in and ask," I say. I glance at Rose before focusing my gaze on Cal, who looks less pleased than I am about returning to the room. As it is, he finds a first-aid website on his phone and reads over the CPR instructions twice before he lets me venture inside.

"ROSE, YOU STAY NEAR THE DOOR," CAL INSTRUCTS AS SOON AS WE'RE ONCE more in the room. "If anything starts moving, you *get out*. Got it?"

"I've got it," Rose grumbles.

He nods at his sister and turns to me. "And you stay away from the door. We don't need you barricading yourself in again."

"Yes sir," I say with a weak salute before I stagger to the wall.

"Okay," Cal says. He looks around the room like he's trying to decide what to do. Then he does a half-shrug and faces the nightstand. "Grandpa, we're back. We need to know where your… treasure, or whatever, is located. Is it in the house?"

The ghost nods, and the pages start turning in my mind. I wait for Cal to continue his questioning until I remember he can't actually see the ghost.

"Yes," I relate, and Cal glances at me before turning

back around.

"Where in the house?" he asks. "Upstairs?"

The ghost shakes his head, and I mimic the motion while trying to focus on the search behind my eyes. Cal is facing away from me. But his sister catches my movement.

"He says no," she tells her brother. "This is so cool."

"*Rose*," Cal warns. Then he returns to his questioning. "On the main floor?" Another no, conveyed in a chain from the ghost to him. "The basement?" Cal asks.

Pain flares. I grip my arm, biting back the cry and willing my brain to work faster.

"He doesn't look good," Rose says.

"That means we're on the right track," Cal replies in a stony voice. "In the basement. Where—"

The words appear like images in my mind, two small snippets from old, dusty books. "Ambry," I choke out. "Amati."

"What?" Cal spins and crosses to me. I didn't realize my head was drooped again, but he lifts my chin and suddenly it's a fraction easier to breathe. "Ambry and Amati. Did I hear that right?" I nod—try to nod—and Cal glances at his sister. "What the hell does that mean?"

"An Ambry is like a cupboard," Rose says.

"How do you know that?" Cal asks.

"One of our awful ballet recitals was at a museum," she says. "I was bored. I read all the plaques."

I smirk, although I'm not sure if the motion actually makes it to my face.

"Okay," Cal says. "So… it's in a cupboard in the basement?"

The pain flares again, and my eyes close as I choke out the word with a groan. "Amati."

"Amati," Cal repeats.

"That's not a cupboard," Rose says.

"No, it's not," he agrees in a thoughtful voice. "Amati, Amati. Amat—*oh*." He must turn away from me because his voice grows dimmer. "Andre Amati?" he asks.

The pain around my neck swells and my chest stings with the scattering sensation of needle pricks. My eyes flutter open to find the ghost in front of me, hazy but bright. I cough, but I can't even do that properly. The picture over the bed rocks against the wall and falls off its nail, while I get my first real waft of the ghost's smell—a sharp, rotten pinewood stench.

"Cal?" Rose says, sounding scared. I can't keep my eyes open. Even with the pain and the smell, they slip closed once more.

"The music room!" Cal exclaims. His voice grows closer. "Andre Amati invented one of the first true violins. The treasure must be in Grandpa's music room." I feel a hand against my face, and then am arm sliding under my back.

"There isn't a music room," Rose says.

"No," Cal agrees. "But there used to be. Help me grab him. We've got to get downstairs."

They drag me out into the hall, and once more I cough and splutter as air rushes back into my lungs.

"That can't be good for him," Rose says. "Like, that's gotta kill a lot of brain cells."

"Shut up, Rose," Cal says, sounding very much like he wants her to be wrong—but is not entirely sure she is.

"I'm fine," I rasp as I try to sit up again. I'm not even sure when I fell to the ground this time. "I've got loads of brain cells to spare. Besides, we're Senders. It's different."

"You'd better be right," Cal says. He gives me a pointed look, then helps me to my feet. "The rec room in the basement used to Grandpa's music room," he explains to both of us as we move. "So, apparently, the treasure is there. Trouble is, we've got to get down there without anyone seeing us."

"I'm on it," Rose says with sudden determination. She throws her braid back and goes into a full-on march down the stairs.

"She's a pain," Cal says as he does another check over to make sure I haven't suddenly sprouted a new batch of stab wounds. "But she's helpful."

"She is that," I agree. I grab his arm, and we head down the stairs behind her, staying far enough back that she can go into the living room before we get to the bottom landing. Someone questions what the noise was upstairs, and Rose answers with convincing innocence that there was nothing upstairs at all.

When the party's attention is firmly on her, we sneak the rest of the way down the stairs. Once in the foyer, Cal grabs my hand to pull me in the opposite direction from the living room, through a dark sitting room and back towards the kitchen. He checks to make sure the coast is clear before leading us to the basement stairs, and we head down to a rec room that matches the house's old age with its beige carpet and wood panelled walls. The air is stale and a little musty, and the old sofa and chairs are worn from use, though they look comfortable enough to sit on—which I do, trying to catch my breath while Cal surveys the room.

"This was Grandpa's music studio while he was

alive," he tells me as he looks around. "It's never really been used since he died. And I don't remember much of the room from before—except that he kept his violin's accessories in that cabinet."

The cabinet he's referring to is hung against the far wall, not exactly hidden but sort of blending in with the wood of the panelling behind it. I don't know if this is the secret spot the ghost had in mind. But I bloody well hope it is.

Cal opens the cabinet just as Rose bounds down the stairs.

"Mom and Dad think you two went off to be angsty teenagers together," she says with a happy smile. "I told them you never came inside."

Her brother sighs. "Thanks, Rose." I can hear the dejection in his tone, the disappointment that his parents undoubtedly believe we're a couple of bratty teens who can't be civil enough to attend Grandma's last Christmas party. I understand how he feels. I'm not thrilled about his parents thinking I'm so antisocial I can't even attend a single function while being a guest in their home.

"Did you find it yet?" Rose asks, oblivious to the heavy mood of the moment. She crosses the room as Cal pulls open the cabinet.

"This is where he kept everything," Cal says. He looks at the empty shelves of the cabinet and shrugs. "But there's nothing here now."

"It's supposed to be hidden," I remind him. "Maybe there's a false backing."

Cal frowns at the cabinet before carefully knocking the wall. He moves his fist along, tapping against the solid wood at the back of the shelves.

"There's nothing behind here, either," he says as he moves his hand. "It's just an empty—"

He knocks on a hollow spot, then turns to me while Rose moves to his side.

"Break it, Cal!" she says.

"Ghosts and their damned walls," he mutters.

I smile as I get up and join them by the cabinet. "Maybe you don't have to break it. If this was intended as a hiding spot, perhaps he made it accessible somehow."

"I can't see any seams," Cal says while I look in beside him. I don't see anything, either, but when I run my fingers along the woodgrain, I can feel a small slit cut into one side.

"Here," I say. I press on the wood, feeling for which side will give. Neither do, so I follow the invisible seam down to the bottom of the cabinet, where Cal picks up on what I've started to uncover.

"There's a latch," he says. His fingers graze mine as he reaches in to grasp the cabinet's bottom edge. Pulling it upward, the cabinet rocks a little before the latch undoes and a portion of the bottom lifts free. Underneath, along the cabinet's bottom shelf, is a hollow of wood.

Inside the hollow is a small, hidden box.

CAL PULLS THE BOX OUT OF THE CABINET.

"Woah," Rose says from his other side. "I didn't think we'd *actually* find anything. You two should open a detective agency. Solving mysteries by talking to ghosts. You'd make a fortune."

"*Rose,*" Cal mutters, while I smirk.

"Silver and Rhoades, Spirit Sleuths?" I tease. "Maybe that's what the Oracle should be teaching us. Would make for more interesting courses over the summer."

"Lock picking and tactful demolition would be handy skills," Cal agrees as he considers the box. "So… do we open it?"

"We should," I say with a grimace, "but probably in front of the gh—your grandfather."

Cal's eyes settle on mine, and our stare lingers a moment before he nods.

"Okay," he says. "Let's get back upstairs."

We make it through the kitchen and around to the

foyer without interruption. But my hand just manages to grip the garland-wrapped banister of the main staircase before we're halted by a voice.

"What are you three doing?"

All three of us turn to see the sight I most dread in any social situation like this. Cal's mother is watching us from inside the living room, her expression cold with barely contained fury. Behind her, the rest of the room—the whole damned party, apparently—quiets and shifts so they can stare too. So much for Rose's lie. If they've seen us running up the stairs now, there's a good chance they know her story from earlier is a load of bollocks.

Cal's cheeks flush with pink, a color probably matching the shade of my own face.

"What are you doing?" his mother asks again in the short, clipped way of someone already convinced of the truth and well beyond the point of persuasion.

"We, uh… we just…" Cal stammers, looking as horrified by the attention on us as I am. A swell of breathless cold wraps around me, but I'm so preoccupied by the expectant silence of the crowd that it takes me a moment to realize that the ghost is nudging me on. I glance down at the box still gripped in Cal's hands. Then I awkwardly clear my throat as I try to pull in a big enough breath to speak.

"We found this," I say, pointing at the box and hoping the ghost hasn't led us on some wild goose chase. Cal raises his arms with a nod, his eyes hardening as he tries to adopt an air of determination.

"Yeah." He steps off the bottom stair and heads for the living room, Rose and I trailing behind in a meek show of togetherness. "We were down in the… uh…

well, we…" he sighs and walks to the woman who must be his grandmother. "I think this is probably meant for you."

The woman looks less annoyed than confused, and it occurs to me for the first time that Cal and I are still in our winter coats amidst all the party guests. I hate this, and I'd love to slip away completely unnoticed now that the attention has shifted. I would, if it didn't mean leaving Cal here to fend for himself.

"Is that…" As Cal gets closer, the woman's eyes focus on the box. At first, she continues to look perplexed by what is happening around her. But then there's a spark of recognition, and she breathes in with an audible rasp. "Is that Callum's box?"

The question throws me until I remember that Cal was named after his grandfather. My Callum nods, and his grandmother takes the box from his outstretched hands. She opens her mouth as she lifts the lid, likely to ask where he found it. But no sound comes out for a long moment as she realizes the box isn't empty.

I sidle up next to Cal, close enough to glimpse the box's interior. Two items are nestled inside. One is a silver pocket watch with an image—I think a violin—etched on its front. The other is something small wrapped in green paper and topped with a golden bow.

Cal's grandmother pulls out the wrapped present, tears streaking her cheeks as she places the box on the mantle behind her.

"That is your grandfather's repair box," she explains as she peels back the present's green paper. "He kept things there that needed fixing. But I couldn't find where he put it after…"

She trails off as she unwraps the gift. Beneath the paper is a black velvet jewelry box and, resting inside, is a gold necklace inlaid with small jewels that form the shape of a flower. The woman puts a hand to her mouth, her eyes squeezing closed. When her eyelashes flutter open again, she lets out a happy sob.

"My mother had a necklace that she handed down to me," she says. "I wore it all the time. But then the chain broke, and one day, one of the jewels came out of its casing. I put it in my jewelry box so it wouldn't get damaged any further. Then it disappeared. For years, I've wondered—Callum must have taken it to be set in a new casing as a present. But he… he died before he could give it." She taps her mouth with her palm in a motion of happy disbelief. Then she looks at her grandson with a peculiar glint in her eyes—maybe understanding for the first time that he's not making all this ghost shit up—and thanks him.

Cal nods before turning to look at me. But as his body shifts, so too does my attention. My eyes cast to a spot behind his grandmother, where the ghost of his grandfather has appeared so suddenly, I haven't had time to feel any incoming changes to the air or pricks of pain along my scars. In one swoop, every one of my old wounds flare like I've just caught on fire, the scorching sensation so complete even my chest aches. But it's not the searing pain that troubles me. It's the vibration that's starting up from the floor—the brightness of the room as the ghost gets ready to exit this party once and for all.

I want to move, but I'm rooted to the spot, stuck with indecision over what course of action will bring me the least amount of pain and mortification. Luckily, Cal's senses are not as plagued as mine, and he understands what is going on. When his grandmother turns to another partygoer, asking them to help her with the necklace, Cal grabs my arm and pulls me out of the room. His parents call his name, but Rose steps in and attracts their attention as we head for the front door.

Cal pulls open the door and pushes me outside, where the sky is cold but alive with floating flakes of white. I breathe in what I can of the frozen air before I glance back to see him standing on the threshold of the doorway. His eyes are closed, his fingers pressed lightly to his temples. As I watch, a soft, contented smile curves his lips. I know the look now gracing his features. It's the one he wears when he's deep into his music, lost in symphonies or concertos from composers long-since dead.

I don't need to ask what he's listening to now. The house is getting bright, and a spirit is about to cross over to the other side. If Cal's hearing one last song, I can make a damned good bet as to what instrument is being played—as to who the player is.

I stare at the beautiful boy in front of me until the vibrations start to stretch beyond the house's walls. Then, gently, I call his name.

"Cal?"

Cal doesn't look startled by my voice. He opens his eyes, his smile growing as he bounds outside to take my hand so we can run as far from the house as possible.

WE END UP IN A FIELD SOMEWHERE ABOUT A BLOCK AWAY FROM THE GHOST.
Lights gleam on other houses to our backs, but in front of us there is nothing but the snow. I have no idea what havoc the spirit's passing will wreak on the party-goers. But I think Senders experience releases differently than other people, and my guess is that the house might suffer a power surge while the people within it stay conscious. I hope that's the case, anyway. Otherwise, we might end up in more trouble than we probably already are.

Not that it feels like trouble right now. Not that it ever feels like trouble when I've conquered something with Cal.

When we get onto the snowy field, Cal turns to me. Without even a beat of hesitation or question about everything that just occurred, he begins unwrapping the scarf from his neck so he can rewrap it around my own.

"I'm sorry about tonight," I say as he stands close, looping the scarf and positioning it so my old wound is not in sight. My heart pounds while he does it, the movement so casual but speaking so much of how well he knows me—of how much he cares.

"You have nothing to be sorry for," Cal says. "We don't get a choice in when spirits show up." He finishes with the scarf and looks at me, his eyes bright as he laughs. "If anything, you performed a bit of a Christmas miracle. You found the jewels. You released my grandpa." He plays with the edge of the scarf, his smile softening. "I heard him, at the end. I got to hear him play again. That makes for a Christmas wish come true."

I hate Christmas. Except for right now. Because knowing I helped Cal and his family makes the whole aggravating season worthwhile. I thought facing a ghost tonight would ruin everything, but it hasn't. Because anything that makes Cal smile like this is worthwhile. I'd face a thousand ghosts if it would make him happy. I'd face any kind of torture to give him a gift like this.

My breath hitches, not like a ghost is near but like my chest is so suddenly swollen I have to remember to force in more air. I'm too full. I can't hold back the truth any longer. And it turns out my body is quicker than my mouth because, before I've even started to speak, my heart ticks into a full gallop, my palms dampen with sweat, and every single part of me buzzes with a grandiose nervousness I've never experienced before.

"We'll stay out for a little while," Cal says, while my body goes into overdrive and I struggle not to get lightheaded all over again. "We can walk around, if you like, or—"

"Cal," I say in a breath too quiet for him to notice. His head turns to the right as he surveys the area to see if there's anywhere for us to go.

"—or we can go back, if you think enough time's pass—"

"Callum."

The use of his full name stops him. He looks back at me, his eyes curious. "Yeah?"

"I just…" After jerkily calling him to attention, my lips grow thick and I can't seem to make an actual sentence. "Tonight. This trip, it… I wanted to let you know… I just… it's just…"

"Meander?" he asks, and his voice is so damned gentle and sweet, it's enough to make what I'm trying to say come out in a ridiculous rush.

"I love you."

The stupid words sound terrible, all hurried and mumbled and not even remotely romantic. I wouldn't be sure Cal even understood them except for the fact that his eyes go wide and, under the big winter coat he wears, I can see his own breath hitch. I watch him, determined not to speak because I know he'll need time to process what I've said. But I've never done anything like this before, and my resolve to not be an idiot only lasts about one and a half seconds.

"You need time," I say in as big a hurry as I've said everything else, "and you don't… it's fine if you don't—"

"Meander." Cal cuts me off as he steps in closer to me, his eyes searching every part of my face as his smile grows. "I love you too."

"I…" I want to say something extremely smart and

memorable, but all I can sodding manage is a pathetic, "yeah?"

Cal laughs. "Yeah," he says with a nod. "Yes."

And then it's suddenly like I'm weightless, like the solidity of me has evaporated and turned to the consistency of the powdery snow. But it's okay because Cal is still solid, and I grab his waist and tether myself to him with the anchor of a kiss. And we've done this a *lot* since I arrived in Canada, but this one feels slightly different from all the others. Because it says everything neither one of us is able to properly articulate. Because it makes the moment worthy of being *a moment*, one I know I will never, ever forget.

When we pull back, Cal rests his forehead against mine for a moment, both of us smiling and holding each other and living in a world where only the two of us exist. He trails a cold finger down my cheek and along the scar that no longer hurts. Then he raises his head, eyes shining as he takes a step back.

"I have something for you." He smiles and reaches down to unzip one of the big pockets in his dad's coat. "It's not wrapped… I got it the day you arrived, and I haven't had any time to wrap it. I was going to give it to you tomorrow, but after tonight… it seems fitting you get it a little early."

He pulls something square out of his pocket, and by the time I see the first corner of the box my eyes are already stinging because I know exactly what it is. Cal hands me the chocolate orange, and I try not to let my hand shake as my fingers close around it.

"Merry Christmas, Meander," he says.

I stare at the chocolate, my throat tight as I struggle to keep from bursting into bloody tears. With a hard swallow, I look up and force myself to smirk.

"I hope you don't expect me to share this with you," I say in as dry a voice as I can muster.

Cal grins before pooling his face into a serious mask. "I wouldn't dream of it. It's all yours."

And despite my best efforts to keep it inside, a traitorous tear still rolls down my cheek. Cal steps forward to wipe it away, and I grab his waist again, desperate to get him closer to me. He brings his hands up to my neck, and my other arm hangs over his shoulder, the chocolate dangling from my fingertips.

"You can have as much as you want," I tell him.

He smiles. "And if I want it all?"

"It's all yours," I say, knowing we're not talking about chocolate anymore.

Cal's hand tangles in my hair as his lips come back to mine. For a long time, we stay tangled together, lost in the swirl of falling snow.

THE STORY CONCLUDES
IN BOOK FOUR OF THE ORACLE OF SENDERS SERIES

ENTITY

ABOUT THE AUTHOR

MERE JOYCE is a Canadian author of books for young adults. Her writing includes contemporary tales, high-action mysteries, and her personal favorite—ghost stories. When she's not writing, Mere can be found recommending books as a librarian, or spending time at home with her family. She's also been known to be a selective, yet highly enthusiastic fangirl.

Find her online at:

MEREJOYCE.COM